TRU

one and all · onen hag oll

CORNWALL COUNCIL

First published in 2015 by Five Lanes Press
Contact: info@fivelanespress.com

Contact: author@jennyalexander.co.uk
Website: www.jennyalexander.co.uk

ISBN: 978-1-910300-08-4 (Paperback)
978-1-910300-10-7 (eBook Mobi)
978-1-910300-09-1 (eBook ePub)

Design and typesetting: Zebedee Design www.zebedeedesign.co.uk

DRIFT

JENNY ALEXANDER

five lanes

ONE

The counsellor was called Marigold Bourne. If I'd been talking, I would have told Mr Baginski that I didn't want to see her, but I wasn't, so I'd just gone on looking at his tie. Whatever.

'I know you probably don't want to be here,' Marigold said. 'But your Head of Year felt it might be helpful.' She left a gap, as if she was expecting me to say something. I didn't. 'He tells me you're having some difficulties at the moment.'

We were in the Quiet Room next to the Secretary's office. Outside the window the sky was dark, and everything looked dirty and brown.

'Let me assure you, Jess, that anything we say in this room is just between us two. It's completely confidential.'

The room was bare except for six chairs covered in sludgy red fabric and a low square table. There wasn't anything on the table except a box of tissues, a folder and two gel pens. I looked at the clock on the wall. You could see the minute hand edging round slowly.

Marigold tried a question. 'Does that sound okay?'

Not talking is like being in a plastic box. You can see out, you can hear what people are saying, but nothing affects you. I was all right with that, it wasn't a problem, and I didn't see why they couldn't just leave me alone.

'Mr Baginski tells me you've been missing a lot of school lately.'

I thought, In a minute she'll say this is a very important year for me; if I don't make a good start on my A-Levels I won't be able to apply for any decent universities. She'll say, 'That would be a terrible waste.'

'This is a very important year...' she said. Blah, blah, blah.

She didn't look like you would expect a counsellor to look. A counsellor should be middle-aged, like your mum, and wear a blue cardigan and sensible shoes.

Marigold was way too young, and she was wearing a fluffy pink sweater, light- blue jeans and grey shoes with a silver trim. She had a silver chain round her neck, and small silver earrings. Her voice was kind of silvery too.

'I guess you're finding school difficult at the moment, Jess?'

If I'd been talking I would have said no, school wasn't particularly difficult, it was all the same to me – school, home, school, home... Sometimes I didn't bother to get out of bed because none of it felt important.

'Mr Baginski tells me you seem very quiet, too.'

We sat there, listening to the clock on the wall and the rain falling outside. After a while, when I thought she'd given up, she suddenly took a clean sheet of paper from her folder, put the gel pens on it and pushed it across the table towards me.

'I can see it's hard for you to talk about things just now,' she said. 'Sometimes people find it easier to draw a picture.'

I looked at the gel pens. Green and purple. Why had she chosen those colours?

'Mr Baginski tells me you love drawing and painting,' Marigold said.

Pause.

'I believe you even take Saturday morning classes at the Art School?'

They'd been talking about me behind my back, and they hadn't even got it right. I used to take Saturday morning classes, past tense. I didn't take them any more.

'Well, I guess you might not feel like drawing right now,' Marigold said, but she left the paper and pens on my side of the table anyway.

Tick, tick, tick.

She had another idea.

'You like writing too, don't you, Jess?'

Pause.

'I hear you write fantastic essays and stories.'

Pause.

'Do you think you could write something for me?'

Why would I want to write something for her? I could hardly even write anything to Lexi, and she'd been trying to get me to for ages. Every day after school, she'd been sending me funny updates about what had been going on in Normal Land while I was off on Planet Jess, as she liked to put it:

At morning break that giant suck-up Caroline told Ms Khan that I've been writing rude things about her on my blog! Can you believe it? 'The Staff Room' is the best thing in it, and now it looks like I'm going to have to drop it.

I was starting to wonder why Lexi was still messaging me, considering I hardly ever answered. It wasn't that I didn't want to; I just didn't seem to have anything to say.

'How do you feel about that, Jess?' Marigold said. 'Could you write something for me?'

A door slammed somewhere down the corridor. The clock ticked. The rain spattered across the window-panes. If I focused hard, if I put all my attention into it, I could also hear the air moving in and out as I breathed. There was a small stain on the carpet near Marigold's feet, perfectly round, like a penny.

Marigold shifted in her chair. She leaned forward towards me and, for a horrible moment, I thought she might be going to put her hand on my knee.

'I understand that your brother, Sebastian, died recently.'

10

The air stopped moving for a split second, then started again. The room felt suddenly hot.

'It must be very hard for you.'

I knew what she was trying to do, with her silvery sympathy. She wanted to make me break down and cry. I stared at the stain on the floor, and it stayed a perfect circle; it didn't even wobble.

'What is it now – four months since he died? People can take a long time to get over the death of someone so close.'

Even if I'd been talking, I wouldn't have bothered trying to explain. No one could understand. You might not be here any more, but it wasn't as if you had totally gone.

It was more like you'd just stepped into another room for a while, and you could come back through the door any minute. That's what people don't understand about death. It isn't real. It doesn't mean anything.

Marigold said, 'How old was Sebastian?'

I looked at my hands. She answered herself.

'Just eighteen, someone told me. That's so very young.'

After that we sat there, listening to the time ticking away. I looked at my hands, the stain, the clock, the window. Eventually, Marigold said, 'I know you don't want to talk to me right now, Jess, but I really do feel it would help you to write things down. Will you try to write something for our next session?'

Our next session?

She picked up the gel pens and some sheets of paper, and held them out to me. Like anyone writes with pens. Like computers hadn't been invented.

'Can you just give me a nod?'

I chewed my lip and looked at the floor.

'Well, let's leave it for now then, shall we? Take these, in case you feel like writing later.'

I took the paper and pens because I was never going to get out of there if I didn't. But Marigold still hadn't finished.

'Or here's another idea…' she said. 'What about writing to Sebastian? Could you do that, and tell him how you feel?'

As I left the room, I thought, Maybe.

Maybe I could keep you up to date with what was going on at home, the same way Lexi kept me up to date with what was going on at school. Someone needed to do that for you now, I thought, since you had stopped talking too.

You know what, Seb – I actually quite like writing with these gel pens. Switching between the green and the purple means that if I lay the pages end to end, they look like a long stripy scarf.

The trouble is, now that I've told you about Marigold I can't think of anything else to say. Lexi could do this so much better than me. I just keep going back over old stuff in my head. Stuff like our party. That's still really bugging me because we weren't straight with you about it.

Lexi said the Easter holidays would be the perfect time for a party and we could make out it was all for you. You really did deserve to have some fun before your A-levels, what with taking five subjects and everything.

The beauty of this angle, Lexi said, was that Mum and Dad would buy it too. If we told them the real reason for having a party, they'd go nuts and ground me for a year.

Lexi called it our sex quest. We might have been out with boys before but, now we were both sixteen, we could legally lose our virginity. 'This is our summer of sex!' she said. Not love or passion or romance; she didn't believe in all that mushy stuff.

'The boys in our year are all losers,' she said, 'but if we can get your brother to have a party, your house will be full of fit sixth-formers and we can take our pick!'

I had my doubts on several counts. No offence, but for one thing, I didn't know how many people would actually want to come to your party, considering you were, well, let's face it, not exactly popular.

For another thing, you were still going out with Della from Chess Central, and her idea of a good time was a three-hour think about her next move.

Not to mention Mum and Dad. Even if they let you have a party, they were hardly going to fill the house up with booze and take off for the night, like other people's parents do.

Last but by no means least, you hated parties. I couldn't see how we'd ever get you to agree to it.

But you know Lexi never hears anything she doesn't want to, so she asked me round to her house one Saturday afternoon to perfect the plan. She must have spotted I was dragging my heels because she threw in an extra incentive.

'You've got to come because I've bought you a present!'

So after my art class that Saturday, I grabbed a burger off the van in Coronation Park and detoured down Bugle Street to check out the charity shops on my way to Lexi's.

I found a great present for her in Save the Children – a book called *Anarchism* by some old Russian guy with a bushy beard. I thought it would look impressive on her bookshelf and, knowing Lexi, she might even read it.

I got some new paintbrushes in the craft shop and carried on down the hill to the roundabout. Someone had beheaded most of the daffodils, so they looked like an island of stalks in a swirling sea of cars.

I bet you've never been to the Downlands Estate, Seb. Lexi says no one would go there if they didn't have to. All the houses in all the roads look the same, with a concrete shelf of a porch and a little patch of grass.

I found Lexi sitting on the front step, with Doris lying out on the path, looking fatter and lazier than ever. She didn't even bother to get up and say hello.

'Tilly was just like that when she was having puppies,' I said.

'Ah, yes. The aromatic one!' said Lexi. Well, Tilly was a bit past her prime by then, and she did sometimes smell like old socks.

'I suppose you want to know what your present is?'

She handed me a small carrier bag.

'Is it some kind of joke?' I asked, seeing the look on her face. 'I've got something for you too actually.'

We opened our presents on a count of three. Lexi was really pleased with her book, and I loved my blue hair dye too. It was odd how Lexi was always so keen to help me look like a weirdo – as she liked to put it – when she herself stuck to jeans and a T-shirt, and would never in a million years dye her own hair blue.

I kind of assumed that Lexi was planning to put some streaks in my hair, not do my whole head, so I was a bit taken aback when she glopped the whole tube on, but it was too late by then. I sat there in the kitchen with all this gluck on my head while she made some tea.

'How many people do you think we should invite?'

she said, rifling through the cupboards for biscuits.

She found a packet of cream crackers and stabbed them open with a knife. 'And what about music, any thoughts?'

'Look, Lexi,' I said. 'Seb isn't going to go for this idea. Trust me.'

'Then you'll have to talk him round!'

I don't know if we left the dye on too long, but when we washed it off, my hair didn't look like hair any more at all. As well as being bright blue it was kind of shaggy and all the shine had gone off it, so it felt like a heap of old knitting wool. Lexi stood back to admire her handiwork. 'That is so cool!' Then she laughed and told me she wished she had my bottle.

I wasn't keen on the texture but I really did love the way people turned to stare at me as I made my way home. I kept catching sight of my reflection in shop windows. My hair looked super bright, and the colour totally matched my purple jacket, pink skirt, stripy tights and black ankle boots.

I knew Mum and Dad would freak if they saw me so I sloped straight upstairs to my room to look for a hat. I could hear them in the kitchen, arguing – or, as they preferred to call it then, 'having a discussion' – about world debt. Did you ever read Lexi's accounts of our family arguments on her blog? She used to say that teatime at our house was like Prime Minister's Questions.

There was gunfire rattling out from the living room, which meant Marky was playing on his Xbox. The light was on in your bedroom and the door was ajar.

I thought I might as well ask you about the party straight away and get it over with. You were bound to say no, but then at least I could tell Lexi I had tried. I put my black woolly hat on, tucked my hair up into it and stuck my head round your bedroom door.

I wouldn't normally have gone into your room when you weren't there, but as I turned to go I noticed the box. It was under your chest of drawers. I might not have seen it at all if the light from your bedside lamp hadn't caught the metal clasp and made it gleam in the darkness.

I thought it was mine, and that's the truth, otherwise I would never have picked it up. I mean, I had one exactly like it, and why would you have to hide something under your chest of drawers unless it didn't belong to you?

As soon as I got it out, I saw that it was actually made of slightly darker wood than mine, and the clasp wasn't broken. Nan must have given you one of Grampy's old cigar boxes too, after he died. I wanted to put it back, but I could feel things rolling about inside it when I tipped it, and I wondered what they could be.

I was standing there with your box open in my hand, gawping like an idiot, when you walked in.

You were not pleased. You were really, really not pleased. You grabbed the box off me, making some of the tablets spill out onto the floor.

'What are you doing in here?' you snapped. I was shocked how angry you were. 'Get out! Leave my things alone!'

I tried to explain about thinking it was my box, but you weren't having any of it and the next thing I knew, I was outside on the landing.

A few minutes later, you tapped on my door and came straight in. You were back to your normal self, all quiet and reasonable.

'You're not going to tell Mum, are you?'

'They can't all be for your own use,' I said. 'Are you dealing?'

I couldn't believe I was even thinking such a mad thought, let alone saying it out loud. My swotty brother – sorry, Seb – a drug dealer? I thought I must have strayed into a parallel universe.

'They're not drugs, you idiot! What do you take me for?'

'Well, they're definitely not potatoes!'

You flopped down on the bed.

'Okay, they are drugs, but they aren't that sort.'

'What sort are they then?'

'They're sleeping tablets if you must know. I nicked them from Nan.'

'You nicked them from Nan? Why?'

'Why do you think?'

There was only one reason I could think of why anyone should want to nick sleeping tablets, but it seemed as crazy as the idea of you being a dealer.

You told me you'd been slipping a few of Nan's tablets into your pocket every time you went round there for the last few months. Once you got a whole bottle, and Nan had to go to the doctor and get some more. She thought she had forgotten where she'd put them.

'It's not as if I'm going to take them or anything,' you said. 'I just like having them.'

'Why?'

You shrugged.

'Maybe they remind me not to go there again. Having your stomach pumped is no picnic.'

'What do you mean, "again"?'

'Well, when I was in hospital before Christmas.'

You explained that one minute you'd been lying on your bed watching *All Star Family Fortunes*, chomping your way through a bottle of paracetamol, and the next minute you'd woken up choking on a tube in A & E.

'Who knew that if you take a big enough overdose sometimes your body shuts down and can't absorb it?'

'Mum told me and Marky that you'd had a fit but it wasn't serious.'

'Did she? Oh!'

Maybe, if you have a big enough shock your brain just shuts down and can't absorb it, the same as your

19

body if you take a big enough overdose. I couldn't seem to take it in.

'So... when you were in hospital before Christmas, that was because you'd taken an overdose of paracetamol?'

You nodded.

'A really big overdose?'

'Yes, but as soon as they brought me round, I knew it had been a mistake. I could have died.'

'If you didn't want to die, why did you do it?'

'Like I said, it was a mistake. I thought I wanted to die, but I was wrong. I was just being stupid.'

I looked at you, and tried to imagine you being stupid, but I couldn't, because stupid wasn't you, it was me; I was the stupid one. My thick head was still refusing to understand what you were saying.

I tried to remember the way things had been before Christmas, and it seemed to me that everything had been just the same as normal. You had been the same as normal. If you had felt so unhappy that you wanted to chuck a whole bottle of painkillers down your neck, surely I would have noticed.

'The thing is, I've told Mum I'm over all that,' you said. 'And I am, really. If she knew about the sleeping pills, she'd only worry. You know what she's like. So you won't tell her, will you? Don't tell anyone...'

You made me promise, and then you went. For ages, I just stood there, staring at the door. I couldn't seem to move. I couldn't seem to think. Random stuff came into my head, like when I was seven, and you were in hospital for all that long time, and Marky was just a baby.

I had to stay with Nan and Grampy lots of nights when Mum and Dad were at the hospital with you, and I didn't always want to. I wanted to visit you as well, but I was just being difficult. Like Mum said, I should have been grateful I wasn't the one in hospital having horrible things done to me; I hadn't lost my leg, and I didn't have cancer and infections.

I remembered this one time, Nan and Grampy took me away for four days in the camper van, but I wasn't allowed to tell you in case you felt left out and got upset. Did you ever find out?

Back then, there were lots of things we kept secret from you, and now I understood there were also things that you and Mum and Dad had kept secret from me. But we two had never shared a secret before. This was new.

Now we both knew about your stash of tablets but Seb, I really wished I didn't.

This must be what it was like in the old days, before email and instant messaging, when people wrote long letters to each other and put them in the post. It takes forever to write, and you don't even know for sure it will get through.

But it feels good, it feels kind of spacious, talking to someone in proper big chunks, being able to write it all down without getting distracted. Yesterday, I told you the real reason why me and Lexi wanted to have a party, and how we used you to get lots of sixth form boys round our house.

Oh God, it sounds bad when I put it like that, but it was bad, and all I can say is I'm sorry. Now, I think I'd better tell you about snooping in your room, which was also bad, but I was desperate.

As soon as I'd promised not to tell, I knew I shouldn't have. I could see what you were saying about Mum freaking out, and how there wasn't any point her getting all worked up if you really were over it. But if you really were over it, why did you have a secret stash of sleeping pills? That part simply didn't make sense to me.

Worrying was making me hungry, so I went downstairs to get a sandwich. Mum and Dad were arguing about world debt in the kitchen but they moved on to the more topical subject of Easter when I walked in, seeing as it was Easter Sunday the next day.

'It's really no more than a festival of chocolate,' Mum was saying. 'What message is that sending to young people about healthy eating? No wonder obesity is becoming such a big problem.'

'Obesity has always been a big problem!' Dad said, laughing at his own joke.

Mum ignored him and launched straight into her healthy eating tirade. I slunk about in the background, making hot chocolate with squirty cream and choc toppits to go with my crisp-and-ketchup sandwich.

'You're not going to eat that, are you?' Mum cried, breaking off in midflow.

'Of course not! I'm going to breathe life into it and create a snack monster.'

Dad laughed, Mum rolled her eyes and I hot-footed it out of the kitchen before anyone had a chance to ask why I was wearing a hat. Tilly followed me up to my room and sat gazing up at me like a fat little sphinx while I was eating my sandwich. I let her lick the ketchup off my fingers.

When she was a puppy and I was a little kid, I used to tell her all my secrets. Sometimes she wouldn't be able to sit still long enough, but it didn't matter because they were little kid secrets and not something big like this.

It felt stupid talking to a dog, but I had to tell someone, so I told her about the suicide thing, exactly like you had told me. I said, 'He was lying on his bed watching *All Star Family Fortunes*, which I know is bad, but...'

Surely you needed some major trauma to make you feel like killing yourself? The only thing I could think of was that you and Della had just split up, but you hadn't seemed that upset about it. It wasn't as if it was the first time.

I hoped it had been breaking up with Della that made you lose it, because then you'd definitely be out of the woods now, with you two being back together again now.

'Della might not be interesting or good looking,' I told Tilly, 'but Seb seems to like her.'

I personally thought you could do better. So did Lexi. She once said to me, 'He might not be cool but he's cute, your brother. You know – tall, dark hair, good skin and those black-framed glasses that make him look so clever. You imagine he's working out maths problems all the time or something, and one day he's going to jump up and yell "Eureka!" in the middle of the bus queue.'

You could probably have gone out with Lexi, actually, Seb, except that she usually goes for guys who've got more of a sense of humour.

'He says he isn't going to do it again,' I told Tilly. 'But if that's true, why does he need a stash of sleeping tablets?'

She stretched out flat and put her chin on her paws.

'He says it's a comfort thing,' I said, stroking the grey wiry fur on her back.

I tried to think of something I might hoard, just for comfort, in case of a rainy day, and it came down to chocolate and extra-strong mints. But I always ate them in the end.

I didn't sleep very well that night, I was so worried. I knew I should tell Mum and Dad, and I thought I probably would in the end; I just needed time to get my head round everything.

I decided to buy myself some time by getting rid of the immediate danger and flushing those tablets down the toilet just as soon as I could get into your room. It wasn't as if you could do anything about it – you were hardly going to go and complain to Mum and Dad. I mean, what could you say: 'Mum, Jess's stolen the sleeping pills I stole from Nan'?

I tried sneaking into your bedroom before breakfast while you were in the shower, but the box wasn't under the chest of drawers any more and I didn't have long enough to do a proper search.

In the cold light of day, my hair looked even brighter blue and even less like real hair, so I put my hat back on before I went downstairs. The table was set for breakfast with a heap of toast on one side and a glass bowl full of boiled eggs on the other.

Each place setting had an egg cup on a plate, and each egg cup contained a Kinder Surprise. Easter wasn't exactly a 'festival of chocolate' in our house. Marky grabbed his, cracked it open and started trying to make the toy inside from all its tiny plastic pieces. You were leaning against the wall behind him, reading.

'What's with the hat?' Mum said, glancing up from serving the grilled bacon and tomatoes. 'Don't you know that wearing a hat all the time can be harmful for your scalp?'

I said it was my Easter bonnet. Dad laughed. 'Still, you'd better take it off at the table.'

I took off my hat.

'Bloody hell!' yelled Dad, his eyes popping out of his head.

'What were you thinking?' cried Mum.

Well, I'd always known they were going to make a scene.

Exit dog out of the back door. Mum carefully puts down the fish slice.

MUM: Tell me that's not your hair. It's a joke wig, right?

DAD: It had bloody better be!

JESS: It is my hair, actually. Lexi did it.

MUM: Of course she did!

CHORUS: *Mum and Dad join together in slagging off Lexi.*

The doorbell rings.

MUM: That will be my mother.

DAD: Christ – that's all we need!

Exit Mum. Nobody moves or says anything. Mum re-enters with Nan, a large woman in a red sleeveless top and baggy white trousers with poppies all over them.

NAN: Hello, everybody. Have I missed anything?
          Oh!

She clocks Jess's hair.

JESS: Lexi dyed it for me.
NAN: Well I think it looks lovely, dear.
MUM: Did you know these modern dyes can
          make all your hair fall out?
MARKY: If Jess's hair falls out, can I have it?

At that point the fried bread caught fire and Mum thrashed it to within an
  inch of its life with a tea towel. I offered to help her with the serving-up, but
  she said I shouldn't go anywhere near food with all those chemicals on my head.
  All the way through breakfast, Mum bombarded us with facts about the harmful effects of hair dye, which it turned out could cause everything from blisters to global warming.
  Marky kept scrutinising me for signs of a major moult, and you just sat there with your nose in your book. Nan tried to stick up for me, but Mum bit her head off.
  'If you choose to ignore the health risks at your age, that's up to you, but Jess is under eighteen and she needs some proper guidance!'
  Nan's eyebrows lifted ever so slightly, and she went

back to spreading marmalade on her toast, which totally matched her bright orange hair. Well, they do say things skip a generation.

I was glad you went to the Easter parade with everyone else after breakfast because I wanted a chance to go up to your room and look for the box. I tried to peer behind your stuff and under the furniture without touching anything, but when I couldn't find it I had to actually go through your drawers and cupboards.

It felt horrible and besides, I was freaking out worrying what else I might discover. But I had to stick to it because it was important. I searched every square inch of your room, Seb, and though I tried to put everything back exactly how I found it, I was sure you'd notice.

Then, there it was, behind the neatly folded sweatshirts at the top of your wardrobe, and there they were, the white tablets, rolling about inside it.

By the time I had tipped them down the toilet and put the box back, I was completely frazzled so, to calm myself down, I got chatting to Lexi. But there was really only one subject I wanted to talk about and I couldn't because:

a) you'd asked me to keep it secret
b) I could never entirely trust Lexi not to make a smart one-liner out of private things on her blog if she got carried away.

I was still chatting with Lexi when you all came back, and Nan came straight up to see me. She sat cross-legged on the floor, as usual – did you realise she had taken to sitting like that because she thought it would stop her hips seizing up?

People in countries where they don't have chairs never need a hip replacement, according to Nan. I didn't like to mention that they probably didn't live long enough to need one if they were so poor they couldn't even afford a chair. I sat down beside her.

'We missed you!' she said. 'The bonnets were lovely.'

Listening to her going on about the bonnets, I found myself wondering whether she knew why you really got rushed off to hospital before Christmas – or had Mum and Dad told her that it was just a fit and nothing serious, too?

I could have talked to Nan, but I didn't want to tell her if she didn't already know. I didn't want her to feel the way that I was feeling, if she didn't need to.

She must have noticed I wasn't really listening, so she changed the subject.

'Don't worry about it, Jess. It's not your problem.'

At first, I didn't realise she was talking about the scene at breakfast. She probably thought I'd spent the whole morning stressing about it, which I might have done if I hadn't had something soooo much bigger to stress about.

'You can't change other people,' Nan said. 'And there's no point worrying about things you can't change, is there?'

'But what if you feel like you've just got to do something?'

I was choosing my words carefully. Nan wasn't. On a scale of one to sensitive, she's always minus ten.

'Well, basically you've got a choice: you can either sulk and stew or get a life. I know which one I'd choose!'

After Nan had gone downstairs to help Mum with the roast, I listened to you moving around in your room and I couldn't stand the suspense of not knowing whether you had noticed anything, so in the end I went to see.

I tapped on your door like someone who thought privacy was important and would never snoop around in a person's cupboards and drawers. As I walked in, you reached over to shut your laptop and I caught sight of a big lump on your wrist.

'What's that?'

You shrugged. You said you'd had loads of them. They'd just started appearing a few weeks before, on your body as well as your arms and legs, but they never lasted long.

'Do they hurt?' I said.

You told me no, not really; they just felt weird.

You pushed your sleeve up and we looked at the lumps together. There were two between your wrist and elbow, which were about as big as a marble, and another one up near your shoulder which was wider and flatter.

'Does Mum know about them?'

You shook your head. 'She'd only go nuts.'

'But what if they're something serious?'

You rolled your sleeve back down and grabbed a sweatshirt from the cupboard. End of discussion.

I knew that later I'd start worrying, like anyone would whose brother once had cancer and was now getting lumps. I would add that worry to the other one, about a brother who had once swallowed a bottle of paracetamol and was now stealing sleeping pills and hiding them in his room.

But there wasn't any point in trying to talk to you about it, when you'd made it perfectly clear you didn't want to.

Anyway, you and me never talked, did we? You were in hospital for such a long time that even when you came home, you still felt separate. And that's how it went on, year after year, you and Mum on one side of the invisible divide and the rest of us on the other.

'Did you want something?' you asked.

I panicked because I'd practised my why-I-searched-your-room-and-stole-your-tablets speech and you didn't seem to have noticed that anything was wrong. I had to ad lib and, though I knew it wasn't the right moment, I went with the first thing that came into my head.

'I think you should have a party.'

'A party? Why?'

'You know, before study-leave and A-levels – a last fling kind of thing.'

'I don't like parties and even if I did, I haven't got time to organise one.'

'What if I organised it for you?'

'You've got GCSE's.'

'I know, but it wouldn't take long. Lexi could help me. She's always having parties.'

You looked at me quizzically.

'Go on, Seb! I want to do this for you.'

Your face cleared, like you were having an a-ha moment, and I knew what you were thinking – that maybe I was worrying about those tablets and wanted to do something to make you happy. That made me feel really bad, but it was as if Lexi was right there in the room, breathing down my neck.

'You wouldn't have to do a single thing, Seb. Please say yes.'

You shrugged. 'OK, then. Yeah. Thanks.'

We went down for supper. On the stairs, I told you there was just one thing I would have to get you to do, and that was to ask Mum and Dad. It would be better coming from you because:

a) you were Mum's favourite
b) Dad always went along with what she said when it came to you
c) you hadn't got blue hair.

In Lexi's house they have their meals in front of the TV, even when her big brother Carl's got his mates round, or his ex-girlfriend's visiting with their baby, Bo. That means they only argue about which programme to watch, whereas we sit up at the table and argue about all sorts of things.

Since it was Easter, we ended up having an argument about life after death. Dad was all 'The idea of an afterlife is just a comforting fantasy for people who can't face up to the biological truth.'

I nearly spat my carrots.

'How can you be so patronising?' I said. 'Just because people don't see things the same way as you, that doesn't mean they can't face the truth! Maybe they have a different truth. Maybe the idea of everything boiling down to biology is just a comforting fantasy for people who can't cope with the truth that people have a soul.'

Mum said the idea of people having a soul was just a fairy story we told young children to stop them worrying about dying.

'When you get to my age…'

Shoot me now!

I changed the subject to satsumas, since that was

what we had for pudding. How could you justify carting food halfway across the globe when there was plenty of home-grown fruit in the UK?

From there, it was a hop, skip and a jump to global warming, which was always good, and when it started to get a bit overheated, like the planet, Dad switched easily back to gardening, and what jobs needed doing over the holiday.

'It might be nice to have an early barbecue,' Mum said.

You took your cue.

'Would it be okay for me to have a party before study-leave and exams?'

They looked at you as if you'd just announced your engagement to Annabel the Baboon.

'A party? I didn't think parties were your thing,' said Dad.

Mum was the first one to rally. 'Right! I'd better get onto it. I'll find a venue and help you with the invitations.'

You said thanks, but actually, I had offered to organise it for you.

'Why?' Mum said, eying me suspiciously.

I tried to look offended that she even had to ask.

'Has this got anything to do with Lexi?' said Dad.

I told him Lexi would probably be willing to help me, yes; she was my friend and that was the kind of thing friends did for each other. He looked pointedly at my hair, which was already fading from glorious peacock to muddy carpet; I was kind of going off it myself.

'So, where are you thinking of having this party?' Mum said to you.

You said you were thinking of having it at home.

'In that case, we'll have to lay down some ground rules,' said Dad.

Firstly, he and Mum would want to be there all the time to make sure things didn't get out of hand. Secondly, he wasn't having a load of drunken teenagers rampaging through the house, so we'd have to have the party in the granny annexe. If the weather stayed fine, we could use the garden too.

'Are you sure you still want to do this?' you asked me later, when we were on our own. I told you of course I was – what could possibly go wrong? Except, I thought to myself, rain pouring down, or no one turning up, or only losers coming, or there being loads of drop-dead gorgeous guys who didn't fancy me and Lexi at all.

But generally in life, Seb, I agreed with Nan. I thought there wasn't any point in worrying over stuff you couldn't do anything about, such as lumps and party disasters. You just had to try not to think about it and everything would work out all right in the end.

I thought I didn't even have to worry about telling Mum you'd been building up a stash of sleeping pills, now they were gone, not for a little while anyway. That's how stupid I was.

Writing it all down, writing it to you, makes me feel sad that we never talked to each other like this before. It makes me notice all the things you didn't know about, and wonder about the things you did know, but never told me.

For instance, you missed the preparations for the party, because you were still at Della's from staying over the night before. Well, Lexi came over after lunch that day, and Mum and Dad mostly left us to it.

The forecast was good for the evening, so we set up the drinks table on the patio. We swept out the annexe and put the music close to the French doors, pointing out into the garden where the dancing was going to be.

'Why did your mum and dad build this huge annexe?' Lexi said. 'It looks like nobody's ever used it.'

'They thought Nan might get depressed living on her own after Grampy died.'

'Your nan? Depressed?'

'I know!'

We put tea lights all the way along the path across the lawn and through the butterfly patch, and I suggested putting some in the potting shed too.

'Are we allowed to use matches in the potting shed now?' said Lexi.

We both laughed, remembering the night we'd had a sleepover out there when we were little and Mum had caught us making a fire in the corner from twigs and leaves.

'You mum's safety talk about what happens to skin when it gets burnt gave me nightmares for weeks!'

Me and Lexi used to love sleeping out there on our quilts and cushions, Seb, having midnight feasts by torchlight until the batteries ran out. It didn't matter that the wooden frame was rotten and the windows were green with moss and mould.

Lexi pushed the door open. There were still a few musty cushions on the floor that had been chewed by something and, on the windowsill, an old mug and a Tupperware box without a lid.

We put a row of tea lights on the windowsill, then came back up the garden to check everything and went inside. You were so late back, I was worried you might not turn up at all, and Mum was tutting and looking at the clock as she served up the curry.

Our 'topic for debate' that suppertime, as Lexi called it on her blog, was classical music. Dad said people who liked pop music were ignorant and shallow – which was bold considering he knew everyone at the table preferred Radio 1 to Radio 3.

I said classical music was like a mouldy old corpse, and it would be kinder for everyone if we didn't keep digging it up.

'I've been reading about Schrödinger's cat,' you said, in a random kind of way. 'It's very interesting!'

Della actually did seem interested. Ditto Dad.

'Schrödinger says, if you had a cat and you sent it off into space so no one could see it or touch it or hear it, would it still exist?'

I said of course it would still exist, and Schrödinger ought to get out more.

'Yes, but how would you *know* it existed?'

Give me strength!

Mum noticed the lump at the same time as me. It was peeping out from under your collar. I wondered if it was a new one, or an old one on the move.

'What's that on your neck?' she said.

You didn't have any choice, so you pulled your collar down, and after a thorough examination, Mum made her diagnosis.

'It's probably just stress.'

'That's what I thought.'

'It'll clear up as soon as the exams are over.'

'I know.' You got up then and said, 'We'd better go and get changed, Della.'

'I'm sure there's really nothing to worry about,' said Mum.

But the minute you were out of the door, she was all 'Oh my God! What if there's something really wrong with him? What if the lumps get worse? What if he gets one on his hand and can't write in his exams? What if he gets one on his face...? I'm going to make him an appointment!'

Me and Lexi went to get ready for the party, then sat with our backs against the end wall under the climbing cherry, while we waited for people to arrive. It was such a lovely warm evening, wasn't it?

'It's like the garden of Eden,' Lexi said. 'And we're about to eat the forbidden fruit!'

We hadn't discussed the finer details of our plan, and I was a bit taken aback. I had imagined we were going to get some boys to go out with that night, with a view to actually 'doing it' later. It suddenly occurred to me that Lexi might be thinking of going all the way right there and then, in our garden.

If Lexi got laid under the fruit trees and Mum and Dad decided to go out on patrol, that wasn't going to do much for her approval rating, which was already close to rock bottom. But what if it was me they stumbled over in the dark, getting it on with one of your sixth-form mates...?

It didn't bear thinking about. Dad had made enough fuss about walking in on me and Jason a few months before, and we hadn't even been doing anything because:

a) Jason had been in my class for ever, and he felt more like a mate than a boyfriend

b) the snooker was just coming to a particularly exhilarating climax.

So anyway, back to the party. You'll remember Mum and Dad were holed up in the living room with a heap of old videos and a bucket of popcorn, and poor old Tilly had to stay in too because they said the noise might frighten her.

Marky and his mate, Darius, were messing about with the camera, taking pictures of everything for 'before and after' shots. You were in the annexe with Della, probably still talking about Schrödinger's cat.

The wall under the cherry trees was warm against our backs. Marky and Darius took some photos of us, and then moved on to get some 'before' shots of the potting shed.

Suddenly, people began to arrive. They came all at once, as if on some kind of secret signal. Loads of sixth formers turned up, and about a dozen others, mostly guys, from Chess Central.

But the problem was, they all knew each other and we were too shy to try and break in and introduce ourselves, so we ended up dancing with each other at the far side of the lawn, drinking beer from a bottle and trying to look interesting.

When it started to get dark, Lexi and me lit all the tea lights, which at least gave us something to do. The fairy lights were in a heap under the drinks table, so we untangled them too, and cleared up some of the empties so that it looked less like a recycling dump.

There was a guy I really liked the look of sitting all on his own on the edge of the patio. I sat down beside him.

'I'm Jess.'

He said, in a not at all friendly way, 'Do I know you?'

Lexi was standing by the drinks table talking to a tall skinny guy with really close-cropped ginger hair, probably dazzling him with her sparkling brainpower. Marky took a picture of them, but they didn't seem to notice.

No one was taking any notice of Marky and Darius any more. Early on, people had been trying to get them drunk for a laugh, but though they were only nine they weren't stupid. I saw them head off towards the trees, like David Attenborough on a mission – 'After dark, the forest comes alive...'

When I looked again, Lexi and the ginger beanpole had gone. Some people were going through the bottles looking for one that wasn't empty. There was a crash, as some of them slewed off the table and hit the concrete.

Everyone just stood there looking at the broken glass, and I was glad when you came looking for me with some girl who had wet herself because she was too drunk to unzip her jeans.

'Can she borrow some of yours? You look about the same size.'

I don't think it was unreasonable of me to say no. I mean, nobody would want to lend their jeans to an incontinent person, would they? But it probably was a bit harsh of me to tell her she'd soon dry out.

'Lexi's gone off with a tall skinny guy,' I said. Straight away you knew who I meant. 'That's Monk.'

'Why's he called Monk?'

'Don't know. But he's okay.'

That girl was a walking warning so I filled my empty beer bottle surreptitiously from the outside tap so I wouldn't get any more drunk than I already was and went to look for somewhere to sit down.

Most of the candles under the trees had gone out, and I could hear people fumbling in the dark. I got to the potting shed and tried to push the door open. A voice inside said, 'Piss off.' So I went to sit under the climbing cherry, on my own.

Nan says that if you want something one hundred per cent that means you're much more likely to get it. Well, Lexi was one hundred per cent committed to this sex quest, and it looked like she had got what she wanted. But if I was honest, I didn't want to just have sex.

I wanted to fall in love first. Was that stupid, like Lexi said? Was it an 'outmoded illusion'? She said we couldn't just sit around these days waiting to be swept off our feet by a knight in shining armour.

'They don't sell shining armour on the High Street, you know.'

I was aware of someone standing close by. How long had he been there? For that matter, how long had I been there? I had no idea.

'Mind if I join you?'

I couldn't see him very well, just a smudge of blond hair and white shirt in the dark, but he had a lovely deep, sexy voice.

'Tris,' he said. 'And you are?'

'Jess.'

'Nice to meet you, Jess.'

He offered me his hand. It was warm, and his touch made me notice how cold I was.

'You're freezing!' Tris said.

He put his arm around me, to warm me up. I liked the smell of his body under the soft cotton shirt, which looked designer, so he was either loaded or knew his way around the charity shops, like me. I turned my face towards him in case he wanted to kiss me.

Then suddenly everything fell apart, like a dream that's just getting good when the alarm goes off. Most people seemed to be going on to a club except you and Della and a few of your Chess Central mates, who were making coffee in the kitchen.

Lexi tagged along with Monk, and Tris still had his arm round me, but we only got as far as the front gate, before Mum came out and hauled us back in.

It was soooo embarrassing. She said me and Lexi were too young to go clubbing, 'Anyway, look at the state of you!' I wished the ground could swallow me up. Or swallow her up, even better.

Lexi wrote her mobile number on Monk's hand, and I wrote mine on Tris's. I don't remember if he asked me to, or if I just did it because Lexi had.

On the up-side, Lexi made it to the bathroom before she threw up, but on the down-side, she was fast asleep as soon as her head hit the pillow, and I wasn't tired at all. I didn't even feel tipsy any more. I just felt happy.

I kept thinking about Tris, his wonderful voice and the warm smell of him when he'd put his arm round me.

And I thought about you. You seemed to have really enjoyed your party and, though Mum says I only ever think about myself, you know what Seb? That made me feel really happy too.

What woke us up in the morning was that Lexi got a text. It was from Monk. It said, 'I think I'm in love!' I felt sorry for him because Lexi didn't have a romantic bone in her body. She tossed the phone back into her bag.

'He's keen,' I said. 'Aren't you going to reply?'

Lexi gave me one of her 'poor child' looks and

got out of bed. The curtains were open and the sun was streaming in. Outside, the garden looked like a war zone.

'Fancy a fry up?' I said.

By the time she came downstairs I had sausages and waffles sizzling under the grill and some oil heating up in the frying pan for eggs and fried bread. The kitchen was full of the smell of cooking.

She slumped down into a chair.

'Who was that boy you gave your number to? I didn't see you with him at all.'

I said we'd actually been down the end of the garden for ages.

'So what's his name, what's he like and is he a good snog?'

'Tell me about yours first. Why's he called Monk?'

'Pass,' said Lexi. 'He doesn't behave like one!'

'So...?'

'Nine and a half.'

Mum came in before I could get all the details. She asked me to put some more sausages on for her and Dad. Marky and Darius came foraging for cereal, on their way through to watch TV.

'We got some interesting pictures last night,' Marky said as they were leaving.

Darius laughed. 'Some *very* interesting pictures!'

'I'll have to look at them later,' said Mum.

Lexi flashed me a look that said, 'Not if we get there first!'

Dad came downstairs. 'Where's Seb?'

'He isn't up yet.' (Mum)

'Do you think he enjoyed his party?' (Dad)

'Yes – but not too much, I hope.' (Mum, anxious)

'He's got to have a life.' (Dad to Mum, somewhat impatient)

'We'd better talk to him about sensible drinking.' (Mum, completely ignoring Dad)

I don't suppose you ever noticed this, but a good talking-to for me consisted of finger-wagging, shouting and drastic sanctions, whereas when you were on the receiving end it was all, 'Sebastian – we're sorry to have to remind you about this, but you really do have to look after your health, and you shouldn't drink too much or you could get unsteady on your foot and take a nasty fall...'

It was stupid because it was ages since you got the all-clear from your cancer, and that foot was part of you now, just like your real one. You didn't even walk with a limp, and no one who didn't know would ever guess you wore a prosthesis.

As soon as you walked in, Mum delivered a warning shot.

'Morning, Seb. Did you have a good night?' Meaning: Were you drunk and have you got a hangover?

You made a brilliant deflection.

'Della doesn't want to go out with me any more.'

Mum abandoned the drink lecture right there.

'Doesn't want to go out with you? What do you mean? What did she say?'

'She said she thinks we haven't got anything in common, and she's leaving the chess club.'

Mum said you couldn't be expected to help with the clearing up when you'd had such a horrible thing happen to you, so as soon as we'd finished eating you disappeared up to your room.

Maybe you were pleased with yourself for swinging it, but it only took ten minutes to bag up the empties and shove them in the boot of the car for Dad to take to the recycling, and the litter-pick afterwards was fascinating. Whoever told me to piss off in the potting shed was practising safe sex and so was someone else under the pear tree.

While Lexi and me sifted through our findings like the Time Team on a dig, Marky and Darius were sorting out their photos in the granny annexe.

'You've been busy,' Lexi said when we went to see how they were getting on.

The whole of one wall was covered with pictures. The 'before and after' theme wasn't just for the annexe and garden but also for the guests. There was *Pretty girl in her own jeans* before, and *Drunk girl in Seb's jeans* after. There was *Lexi talking to tall guy by the drinks table* before, and *Lexi in love* after.

'Great pictures – not so sure about the captions,' said Lexi.

There was *Seb and Della talking about physics in*

the annexe , and *Seb and Della going upstairs. Dad setting up the drinks table* and *Dad taking the empties to the bottle bank.*

There was *Jess trying to chat up unfriendly boy* (oh, God!), and *Jess with blond guy under climbing cherry.* I didn't remember Marky taking that one at all.

But Tris looked gorgeous in it, just like I imagined as we sat there in the dark. He was looking down at me, and I was looking up, and any minute now we were going to kiss. I wanted a copy, but I wasn't going to ask for one while Lexi was around.

'That's the guy who played the lead in the school play,' Lexi said.

It was! I remembered now. And he chose me!

Mum called from the patio, 'Do any of you want some juice or coffee?' We heard her coming down the garden.

'She's going to make you take some of these down,' I said to Marky.

I mean, it can't look good for an office manager and a healthcare professional to have pictures on display of people getting drunk and groping each other in their garden. Not to mention the one Darius got through the potting shed window (though it was quite blurred).

Mum brought a tray of drinks and digestives. She scrutinised Marky's display. 'Some of these will have to come down,' she said. 'We can't have any of Seb and Della – that would be too painful for him now.' Then she went. We all just looked at each other.

'Your Mum's so weird,' Lexi said.

Strong coffee is supposed to wake you up, but it didn't work, and Lexi went home to bed. Marky and Darius went back to the computer to take Della out of the Seb-and-Della shots, and see if they could make you look happy on your own. They wanted to have some pics of you on their party wall. It was your party after all. I took the tray back to the kitchen.

'Where's Seb?' I asked Mum.

'In his room. Why?'

'No reason. I just wondered how he was.'

'His girlfriend dumped him – how do you think he is?'

'She's always dumping him.'

'Talking of girlfriends,' Mum said, 'you're too young to go out with that boy.'

'What boy?'

'The one in the photos.'

'Right.'

'Why would a boy who's about to go off to university be interested in a Year 11? Think about it.'

Was she saying I was immature?

'Don't stare at me like that,' she said. 'You look ridiculous.'

I didn't want to argue and anyway, actions speak

louder than words, so I just walked out. I could hear you moving about in your bedroom. Tilly was lying on my bed having a snooze and I curled up beside her. She smelt all warm and doggy.

'You know what Mum's problem is,' I told her, or maybe I just thought it, I was so tired I couldn't tell. 'She doesn't want me going out with anyone when Seb isn't.'

That's how it was with Mum; everything always came round to you.

Mum needn't have worried about me going out with someone when you weren't because a week later you were back with Della (big surprise) and I still hadn't heard from Tris.

It didn't help that Monk had been texting Lexi 24:7 and every time she got a new text she made sure all of us at school knew about it.

'He must be crazy about you,' Joely kept saying. She can be such a suck-up!

'Or he just hasn't got much else to do,' I said. All you sixth formers were on study leave – lazing around at home in other words (except you, obviously). We had another two weeks before study leave for GCSEs, which made a lot of sense considering we were taking three times as many subjects.

Lexi laughed. It seems that Monk was super-busy

applying for jobs in between doing revision because he didn't want to go to university. This came as a bit of a shock to me. Lexi famously didn't suffer fools gladly. If Monk was both stupid *and* in love, things weren't looking good for him at all.

I wanted to know about Tris. All I'd found out about him so far was that he was drop-dead gorgeous, smelt wonderful and had a sexy voice, which were the most important things, obviously, but they weren't enough.

He must be clever because of starring in the school play and learning all those lines, so Mum was probably right that he was going to university. You could see he was super-confident too.

So did that mean his family had lots of money? Not necessarily, because Lexi was clever and confident too, and her mum had to borrow money off the neighbours when the electric ran out.

I couldn't imagine Tris living on the Downlands Estate, though. I pictured him growing up in one of those big houses on the hill, with a swimming-pool in the garden. Was that why he wasn't texting me, because he was too busy drinking cocktails beside the pool?

By the end of Wednesday, Lexi had stopped asking me if he'd texted and then, just like magic, as I was walking home from school, he did. At last!

want 2 meet up?

I read it again. He wanted to see me! Ha! So much

for 'You're too young for that boy!' Now I had his number, I couldn't wait to text him back, but I made myself hold off until I got home. Actually, I couldn't wait to hear his voice again, but I didn't think it would be okay to answer his text with a call.

I dropped my bag inside the front door and went straight up to my room.

that wd b gr8

Should I finish with just *j, luv j, love j*? Would a few xxx's be all right? I couldn't decide, so I sent it like it was.

I lay on my bed looking at my phone.

Nothing.

I'd been too keen!

Nothing.

I'd been too offhand (no *j, luv j, love j, xxx*)

Nothing.

Nothing, nothing, nothing.

I tried to do some History revision, but I couldn't concentrate, so I switched to *The Catcher in the Rye*. It was supposed to 'speak to young people', according to Ms de Rosa, but it wasn't speaking to me.

Come on phone, come on phone, come on phone!

When it finally rang, I thought it was him, but it was just Lexi. She said she and Monk were going on a date. He knew this great pub on a river; he was going to drive her there! She talked about it like it was something she did every day, something she'd been doing for years.

I'd never tried to get served in a pub and I was pretty sure Lexi hadn't either, but if she didn't think it was going to be a problem... I couldn't help myself.

'What about a double date, you and Monk and me and Tris?'

'I didn't know Monk and Tris were mates.'

'They probably aren't, but we are.'

'So he finally got round to phoning you, then?'

'Of course!'

'All right,' she said. 'It could be a laugh.'

When I went downstairs, Dad had laid the table and was halfway through a glass of red wine.

'Mum's got some bad news,' he said.

What – now? I can't even have five minutes of punching-the-air, my-love-life's-finally-getting-off-the-ground enjoyment?

Mum stopped chopping stuff and wiped her hands on a tea towel.

'You know I took Seb to the allergy clinic today?'

I had known, but I'd forgotten.

'Well, it turns out he's allergic to house dust.'

So we'd all have to do a bit more cleaning. That was obviously bad news for me when I'd only just got a new potential boyfriend, but why were they making such a big deal of it?

'He's also allergic to animal fur.'

And?

'We might not be able to keep Tilly.'

Hey! No – hold it right there! I mean, fair enough

we couldn't keep Tilly *in the kitchen*, but she could live in my bedroom. She was only small and I had plenty of room.

'We can't keep Tilly in the house.'

'So we can keep her in the granny annexe, then.'

Dad shook his head. He didn't look at me.

'We think Tilly might have to be put down.'

'That's stupid,' I said.

Mum said I had to understand that your allergy was already painful and disfiguring, but it could suddenly get worse at any time. It could make you have breathing difficulties or fits, and even put your life at risk.

According to Mum, eating chocolate and dyeing your hair could put your life at risk, as I wasn't slow to point out, but Dad told me he didn't think I understood the seriousness of the situation.

'This isn't easy for any of us,' he said. 'But your mother and I have got to put family before pets.'

Tilly was part of the family! We'd had her since I was five, which meant she was arguably more part of the family than Marky.

'You can't have an animal killed when there's nothing wrong with it. That would be murder. The vet wouldn't do it.'

Mum said, 'Actually, unwanted pets are often put down.'

'Tilly isn't unwanted!'

'You know what I mean.'

I said, 'What does Marky think?' Straight away I knew they hadn't even told him. They were telling us one at a time. Divide and conquer.

'What does Seb think?'

I was sure you'd be prepared to put up with a few lumps if it meant that or killing Tilly. They couldn't even look me in the eye.

'He's only going to be here for a few more months,' I said. 'Then he'll be at university. We could get someone else to look after Tilly in the meantime. Nan could do it.'

Mum said if Nan looked after Tilly you wouldn't be able to go round her house at all, and we'd never be able to go as a family.

'Okay then. What about someone else?'

Dad shook his head.

'Tilly's really old now, anyway.'

Tilly was lying in her basket with her ears down. She knew we were talking about her but she didn't know what she'd done wrong.

'Don't get upset,' Mum said.

Don't get upset?

'We haven't decided anything yet,' said Dad. 'We just thought you should know how things stand.'

There was no arguing with them. They were being mental. They were being horrible. I couldn't stay in the same room with them, so I went to see Nan, and by the time I got there I was fuming. She opened the door and I burst straight in.

'Seb's got lumps, and now they want to kill Tilly!'

'I know,' said Nan, catching up with me in the kitchen. 'I know.'

She got me by the shoulders and sat me down.

'Would you like some apple pie?'

There was a home-made pie on the table that looked as if it had just come out of the oven. It seemed pretty random, but that was always Nan's approach to cooking, wasn't it, Seb? I remember you telling me she gave you macaroni cheese for breakfast and chocolate cake for lunch one time when you stayed over to help with the garden.

I noticed I was starving hungry. Nan had remembered to put the sugar in her apple pie this time, so I had two slices. She knew all about Tilly – Mum must have phoned her as soon as I left the house.

'What am I always telling you?' Nan said. 'Don't meet trouble halfway. It might come to nothing.'

'Your Mum and Dad just haven't had time to think things through. They're having a panic, that's all.'

Yes, of course, that was it! Worrying about your lumps meant they weren't thinking straight. Maybe I had over-reacted, because nobody could actually kill the perfectly healthy dog that they'd loved for ten whole years. When they'd calmed down, Mum and Dad would feel terrible for even thinking about it. As they should.

'A little bird tells me you might have a new boyfriend,' said Nan.

I told her all about Tris, everything, even that he hadn't got in touch for a whole week after the party and I hardly knew anything about him and that Mum thought he was too old for me.

Nan didn't seem to think any of that was a problem. If I liked his look and the sound of his voice and I wanted to see him again, that was enough.

'I'm sure he's lovely,' she said. But then, Nan liked everyone, including Lexi.

The double date was on the Saturday afternoon. I told Mum I was going round to Lexi's house, which was technically true because Monk and Tris were going to pick us both up from there.

I've only just realized, writing this to you now, that you probably didn't even know I'd been out, since you'd stayed over at Della's the night before and by the time you got home everything was kicking off.

So anyway, when they pulled up outside Lexi's house, Tris got out to let Lexi sit in the front with Monk and sat in the back beside me. Nobody said much as we drove out onto the bypass. It was actually all a bit awkward.

Tris and Monk exchanged a few comments about the cricket. Lexi and I could've chatted about our week, but it would have sounded childish talking about school. Anyway, nothing interesting had happened at school since Annabel Harkness got pregnant by the postman (and even that probably didn't really happen).

Tris put his arm round me in the back of the car, and I leaned into him, enjoying the feel of his body, thinking maybe there was no need to talk, because everything was perfect.

Monk mentioned that the pub was called The Globe. Lexi made some comment about it, and he immediately chimed in with a complete list of all the places he'd ever been to in the world plus all the ones he would like to visit one day.

Lexi hadn't actually been anywhere, because her family couldn't afford holidays, but she was famously genius at Geography so she managed to hold her own. The two of them were still talking about travel as we found a parking space and walked round the side of the pub, looking for somewhere to sit.

The pub garden sloped down to the river. All the tables were full, and there were several families on blankets with small kids running around. We picked our way through them and sat down near the long grass at the edge of the water.

I'd been worrying all the way there about me and Lexi getting asked for ID, because that would just be embarrassing, so it was a relief when Tris went in on his own to buy some drinks.

'Have you ever been to the Far East?' Lexi asked Monk, just when I thought he'd finally run out of travel stories, and he was off again. He hardly paused to say thanks when Tris gave him his pint of coke – he couldn't have anything else because of driving.

A fat bee was noisily working some blue flowers behind Monk, weighing them down until they nearly touched the ground, and there were shiny dragonflies hovering over the water.

I wanted Lexi and Monk to stop talking, or at least for Tris to stop listening to them, so that I could say something. But what could I say that would be interesting to him? I couldn't tell if he was really fascinated by German autobahns, Russian border controls, French high-speed trains etc, or if he was just pretending to listen.

He kept looking at me in this really intense way, which felt like an actual touch lightly brushing across the back of my neck and all the way down my spine. He was interested in me even though I hadn't really said anything; maybe if I tried to talk it would only break the spell.

But I was so curious about him. He was wearing a dark grey T-shirt with a waistcoat, which shouldn't have looked good but, on him, it really did. I wanted to know where he got it. I wanted to know everything about him. I thought, Shut up, Lexi! We get that you're clever and witty and interesting, but please, for once in your life...

I asked Tris, 'What are you going to do at uni?' Lexi butted in, 'Way to make small talk!' and Monk agreed. According to them, people were always trying to define each other by their social status. Asking someone what he wanted to study was just another way of saying 'What role are you going to have in society?' It was as bad as asking them what their parents did for a living (there went my next question) or where they lived (and the next).

'I agree,' said Lexi, going into super-smug mode. 'A person is more than their job or postcode...' Monk interrupted her. 'That's the great thing about travelling. It's just you and the open road. No luggage, no labels.' Per-lease!

Lexi mentioned that she'd been reading Kropotkin's book, *Anarchism*, the book I'd given her, and Monk nodded enthusiastically.

'Ah, yes. St Petersburg is one of the places you just have to see. When I was there last year...'

They were as up themselves as each other. I was fed up with Lexi for putting me down – I mean, how were you supposed to get to know someone if you didn't ask them where they lived, and what they wanted to do with their life?

Tris went in to buy another round. He'd hardly given us time to finish the first one, so either he was as riveted by the conversation as I was or else he just liked drinking.

When he came back, I asked him if he played sport and he said yes, but that was as far as it got because Monk started boring for Britain on the history of the Olympics and where Athens fitted in with his travel plans.

It seemed to me that he was just spouting a load of stuff from holiday shows, and most of the places he'd actually been to were on city-break weekends. I couldn't see why Lexi was so impressed by him.

My vodka and coke was strong on vodka, but I drank it quickly because:

a) it helped me get through Monk's travel monologues
b) it meant he would have to go to the bar sooner, because it was probably his round.

'Do you play a sport?' I asked Monk. Looking at him, I didn't think it was likely, and I thought maybe that would shut him up.

'I haven't got time,' he scoffed. 'I've had weekend jobs since I turned sixteen. Some people have to work, you know, not like your boyfriend there.'

He gave Tris a scornful look.

'I don't suppose he'll be getting a job over the summer to earn money for uni like everyone else.'

I suddenly realised that he and Tris didn't only have nothing in common – they probably actively disliked each other.

Tris said he didn't have time to get a job because he was going to Sardinia for four weeks with his family. They had a villa there.

'I'm sorry if that upsets you,' he added.

Sardinia! That took the wind out of Monk's sails all right. He got up grumpily to get the next round. There wasn't any discussion about it, so it looked like he and Tris had decided not to let me and Lexi go inside and try to buy drinks; they'd thought about our ID problem too.

While Monk was at the bar, Lexi didn't bother trying to make conversation with Tris at all, which was rude, but that's Lexi all over. If she doesn't like a person, she doesn't see why she should have to talk to them.

Not that Tris seemed that bothered. He ignored her too, reaching across to run his fingers along the back of my neck as I made a daisy chain, remarking how lovely I looked. I didn't have to see it to know that Lexi was rolling her eyes.

Monk came back with our drinks and we had to sit through another twenty minutes listening to him and Lexi droning on, before Tris suggested going for a walk. Thank God! We all went over the stile onto the riverside path. Tris put his arm round me as we walked along.

Monk and Lexi were talking about money. 'Possession is theft,' Monk said. Lexi heartily agreed. It felt quite pointed, since we'd just found out Tris's family had a villa in Sardinia, and I didn't blame him for pulling back to let them go on ahead.

I thought it was just hard cheese with Monk and Lexi – some people had more money than others:

fact. My family had more money than Lexi's and Tris's family seemed to have more money than Monk's, but there wasn't anything any of us could do about that. They should get over themselves.

We walked along in silence for a while, with the river on our right and the fields on our left. We came to some trees and sat down in the shadows. After a few minutes, Tris lay back.

I picked a blade of grass and chewed the end of it, then stopped, remembering the last time I'd done that, when Lexi and me had been walking on the heath. 'Do you know why grass tastes like dogs' piss?' Lexi had said. Then she'd nodded towards a golden retriever rummaging about in the bushes, and laughed.

'Lie down.' Oh my God – that gorgeous voice ! He reached up and pulled me down beside him.

When he started kissing me, I wanted it to go on for ever and never stop. His lips moved down to my neck, and I didn't notice straight away that his free hand was moving up inside my top. I pulled away a bit. He said, 'What's wrong? Don't you like me?'

I thought he was going to sit up, stand up even, go on with the walk, and not kiss me again.

'Of course I like you,' I said.

We kissed for ages, and then his hand went up my top again and before I knew it, he'd got my bra undone. I liked the feel of him, the taste and smell of him, but we were really close to the footpath and Lexi and Monk might come back any minute.

Anyway, things were definitely moving too fast. He was undoing my jeans. I struggled to sit up. He said, 'I thought you'd had lots of boyfriends. Sorry.'

I couldn't tell if it was supposed to be a put-down. It felt like one, but I was probably being over-sensitive. It could just as well be that he really was sorry for being too pushy.

'I had you down as more of a free spirit, with the blue hair and all that,' he said, as I sorted out my clothes. I decided to take it as an apology.

A middle-aged couple shot disapproving glances at us as they walked by, and I said to Tris, 'It's just a bit public here.' We could see Lexi and Monk coming back now anyway. They weren't arm-in-arm or anything, but they were still locked in conversation. Oh, joy.

All the way back in the car, I kept catching Lexi's eye in the driving mirror. If we hadn't been with her and Monk, it would have been much better. Me and Tris would have talked about subjects we were interested in, not travel and money. I'd have found out about the house on the hill and the swimming pool etc.

Tris would have asked me normal stuff such as what music and TV I liked. He'd have given me that look which felt like a touch on my neck and all the way down my spine, and then maybe we'd have held hands for a while.

We'd have got to know each other a bit before we went for our walk, and when we lay down beside each other, he would have known he had to take his time, and I would have been sure that it was what I wanted.

Lexi and Monk were not like us. They made everything feel cold and business-like. Whatever happened next, I definitely wasn't going on another double date with them.

I didn't want to talk to Lexi but Monk had a Saturday job and by the time we'd stopped off for pizza at the drive-thru he was late for his shift, so he dropped Tris off at the High Street and me and Lexi outside her house.

I don't think Lexi wanted to talk to me either, because she didn't ask me in. We hung around on the pavement for a few minutes, feeling chilly now that the sun was going down.

'So do you think Tris is the one, then?' Lexi said.

I shrugged. 'What about Monk?'

I meant, Are you going to go all the way with him?

She said, 'He thinks Tris is a knob.'

'Charming!'

'Well, you did ask.'

'And I suppose you agree with him, as he's such an expert on everything.'

'It doesn't matter what I think, does it? You're the one who's going out with him.'

Walking home, I couldn't help feeling fed up. It looked like Lexi might have found love when she wasn't even looking for it. Lexi – who thought love was for fools and weaklings.

If things didn't work out with me and Tris, all the

sex quest would have meant from my point of view was that I lost my best friend to a travel bore with a high opinion of himself.

But, as Nan would say, why worry about it? It might never happen. Tris might still turn out to be the love of my life, and Lexi might spot that Monk was a pompous know-it-all and go back to saying love was for losers again. No one ever knew how things were going to turn out in the end.

By the time I turned into our road, I was looking on the bright side again, as Nan would say. The birds were singing their end-of-the-day song in the hedges and front gardens and the yellow street lights were flickering into life.

The first thing I noticed when I opened the front gate was that Marky was still outside, kicking his football against the side wall. Considering he always played on his Xbox after supper, I asked him what was up but he ignored me and carried on kicking.

The second thing I noticed as I went round to the back door was that Mum was doing some gardening. She hardly ever did gardening, did she? – hence the butterfly patch – and besides, it was getting too dark to see the weeds. She must have heard me coming, but she didn't look up.

The third thing I noticed was that Tilly's lead wasn't hanging on the back of the door. Dad must have taken her for a walk, though actually, come to think of it, Dad never took Tilly for a walk.

Something was different in the kitchen. It took me a few minutes to realise what it was. Tilly's basket had gone.

'I thought I heard you come in,' Dad said, appearing in the doorway.

I moved behind the table, in case he was planning to give me a hug.

'Did Mum tell you?' he said.

He sat down at the table and waited for me to sit down too. I didn't.

'We thought about it really hard. But you know, when Seb goes to university, he'll still be here in the holidays, and that's almost half the year.'

He waited for me to say something. I didn't.

'We had to do it, Jessie. We couldn't keep Tilly here in the house, and no one else would have wanted to take her on at her age.'

'What has Tilly's age got to do with anything?'

'Vet's bills can go through the roof with older pets.'

'But we'd have paid them, exactly the same as if Seb hadn't got lumps and Tilly had stayed with us.'

'Anyway,' he said, seeing my face. 'Imagine how she would have felt, being left with a stranger and never seeing any of us again.'

I imagined it. Then I imagined how she must have felt being taken to the vet's (which she hated), put on his table and injected with poisonous chemicals until she was dead.

'You killed her,' I said, in an experimental sort of

way. It sounded wrong. It was wrong! 'You didn't even tell us.'

'We did warn you it might be a possibility, Jess.'

'That's not the same thing as going ahead and doing it.'

Mum appeared at the back door, pulling off her gardening gloves and stamping the dirt off her boots.

'You killed Tilly. How could you?'

She opened her mouth to explain, but I didn't want to hear it.

'Well, I hope you're happy now. I hope Seb's happy now.'

An odd look passed between them, and I realised that they hadn't told you what they were going to do – perhaps you still didn't know what they had done.

'He doesn't know, does he? When were you going to tell him? Or were you just hoping he might not notice?'

We heard your key in the front door.

'How's he going to feel when he finds out Tilly's dead, and you killed her because of him?'

Mum said she hadn't had a chance to talk to you yet, and this wasn't a good way for you to find out about it.

'What are you going to say to him, then?' I didn't try to keep my voice down like she wanted. 'How are you going to dress this up so it seems okay? You know it isn't okay! God help me and Marky if he ever gets allergic to one of us!'

TWO

'How are you feeling now, Jess?'

Marigold left a gap, as if she was expecting me to answer.

'Did you write anything for me?'

It occurred to me that I hadn't brought her gel pens back. Should I feel bad about that? I didn't feel anything. Anyway, there was a new stack of paper beside the tissues on the low table this week, and two new gels, one blue and one orange.

'Did you write to Seb?'

It was still foggy outside, with that smudgy damp fog you get after bonfire night if the weather's very still. Someone had left a pencil case on the windowsill; I wondered who.

'Did you tell Seb how you felt about him dying?'

I suddenly realised I'd got side-tracked – how had that happened? Why had I gone off on all that random stuff about Tris and Tilly, instead of talking about you and me, and what had happened in the months since you'd been gone?

Maybe it was partly about coming clean. I lied to you about the party, and I didn't tell you when I knew that Mum and Dad were thinking about killing Tilly, but I always thought I'd tell you the truth one day – it seemed like we had all the 'one days' in the world stretching out in front of us, back then.

Or maybe I was putting off talking about the other stuff – hanging back from it, like you hang back from a raging fire if you don't want to get burned.

Marigold sat forward a little and re-crossed her legs. She was wearing the same grey shoes with the silver trim, but instead of jeans she had on black trousers with a lilac shirt. Although I could feel her looking at me, I couldn't bring myself to meet her eye.

It was disappointing, because I'd actually been looking forward to seeing her again. Writing to you had been good, and I thought she must know what she was doing.

If I could talk to her, she would know what to say to make things better again, and I thought I would talk to her, but when it came to it, I blanked. No thoughts, no feelings, no words.

'A death in the family is very hard,' Marigold said. 'Especially a suicide.'

Tell me something I don't know.

'It's like a bomb going off. Everything's ripped apart and afterwards, it can take a long time for the dust to settle, so that you can see the extent of the damage, and start rebuilding together.'

Rebuilding? Together?

'There may be a lot of guilt and blame flying around – but it's usually misplaced.'

I was looking at the round stain on the carpet, wondering if a 2p coin would completely cover it. Marigold was talking about her parents.

'They called me Marigold because my mum was planting marigolds in the garden when she went into labour. Our surname is Bourne, so they thought Marigold Bourne was the perfect name for someone who was almost born in the marigolds.'

And this was relevant to me... how?

'I was always teased at school, and blamed my parents for giving me a silly name. It's natural to blame other people when things go wrong, because that's a way of trying to make sense of it.'

Did she think I blamed Mum and Dad for you dying? Was that what she was getting at?

'In the end, of course, I realised my parents had never meant to make life hard for me by calling me Marigold, and actually, it's good now because no one ever forgets my name.'

She was beginning to sound like Nan, always looking on the bright side. It was a good job I wasn't talking or I might have told her that if my parents had called me Marigold, I'd have put myself up for adoption.

Marigold said, 'When someone kills themselves, we don't just blame each other. We also blame ourselves.'

She paused. I stared at the stain. It wobbled. She sat forward a bit. I thought, Don't touch me! The dark stain re-formed into a perfect disk again.

'No one is responsible for someone else's actions,' Marigold said. 'Your brother killed himself. That was his decision.'

Someone knocked and opened the door, glanced into the room, muttered something and shut the door again.

'When a person takes their own life, everyone in the family thinks they should have been able to do something to prevent it,' Marigold said. 'But really they're the last people in the world who could help. They're too close, do you see?'

After that, she fell silent too. I wondered how she could go on sitting there, so calm and still, waiting for me to say something, knowing I wasn't going to. If I'd been her, I'd have drawn a doodle or checked my phone or something.

There was no sound in the room except the clock, working its way round the hour. Twenty-five minutes to go. Twenty minutes to go...

'It's very difficult for me to work with you, Jess, when you can't talk to me about the things that are troubling you.'

Silence.

'I don't know whether it's really worth going on with these sessions at the present time.'

Silence.

'Do you want to come and see me again next week, or shall we leave it for a little while?'

I looked up at her, then quickly looked away. Marigold took a deep breath and sighed it out.

'Okay, we'll meet again next week. Is that what you would like?'

Silence.

'Is that what you would like, Jess?'

I gave a slight nod. I was starting to feel panicky, like someone who was drowning, and the lifeline wasn't quite long enough. There were still fifteen minutes left of the session, and I was afraid that maybe Marigold would change her mind about seeing me again if I didn't start to talk, but I just couldn't.

Ten minutes left.

'I understand it was you who found your brother's body.'

I tried to nod but my neck seemed to have seized up. Marigold said, 'You know, sometimes a shock like that can literally strike somebody dumb.'

When she said that, I remembered the moment the silence fell – that's what it was like, a thick blanket falling down on me, completely covering me, smothering me. I'd never made the connection, but Marigold had.

'I know you can't tell me about it now,' she said. 'But it would be wonderful if you could manage to write something down. Just describing how you found your brother might help to unlock it for you.'

She pushed the paper and gel pens across the table towards me. I leaned forward and picked them up.

'Describe what happened, Jess. Remember to mention how you were feeling. Can you do that for me?'

I felt hot all of a sudden. I wanted to go outside and get some air.

'You don't have to show me what you've written. You don't have to show anyone if you don't want to.'

The minute hand reached the top of the clock. I got up to go. Marigold stopped me.

'Is there anyone you can talk to if you need to?'

So she really did think this might get me talking again, and before next week. Well, there was Nan, I thought. Nan had always been the first person I would go to with my problems. But that was in the old days when I still trusted her advice. Before she told me not to worry about Tilly because it might never happen; before you went and proved that things don't always work out fine in the end.

If I was going to talk to anyone now, it would have to be Lexi. She was still trying to chat to me online every day, even though she was going out with Monk – usually if one of us had a boyfriend we hardly bothered with each other at all.

You notice things when you aren't talking, and I had noticed that though most people were in awe of Lexi, not many people actually liked her. I could probably only like her myself because I wasn't in awe of her. Maybe it was true what she said, that she missed me, and wished we could get back to normal.

Marigold jotted down a number on a piece of paper and handed it to me.

'Give me a ring if you need to.'

She waited while I put it in my phone. I guess it was supposed to reassure me, but it freaked me out. Evidently, she expected my voice to come back just as soon as I had written about how I had found you, and she seemed to think that when that happened I would need to talk to someone straight away.

Okay, here I am. I've got my gels and paper. Everyone else is in bed, and the house is completely quiet.

I've got Marigold's number, but my mobile's set up to phone Lexi. All I have to do is press the button.

If Lexi knew I was writing to you, she'd think it was weird. She reckons a person is just so many cells, and when you die you rot down into worm food and that's it, end of story.

It seems like most people think that way, because when someone dies everyone acts as if nothing unusual or confusing has happened, and no one talks about it at all.

That's how it was when Tilly died. Mum and Dad bagged up her basket and bowls, put a new pot plant in the gap and expected us all to get on with our lives.

Marky started going out on his bike in the afternoons at the time when he used to take Tilly for a walk. You were either round at Della's revising or playing chess on your computer. But Tilly's death changed everything for me.

Up to then, I was like Nan – I trusted that things would always turn out fine in the end, and that people were basically good. What happened to Tilly was not good. She loved us – she needed us, and we betrayed her.

Mum and Dad did a bad, wicked thing. So did Nan, by sticking her head in the sand when she knew what they were thinking about doing. I was ashamed to be part of our family. I didn't even want to be in the same room as them.

I couldn't get my head round what had happened – one minute Tilly had been there, all warm and wiry – you could touch her and see her and smell her (Lexi didn't call her the aromatic one for nothing) – and the next minute, nothing. Gone. Vanished into thin air.

There wasn't even a body we could bury, thanks to Mum. She had left her at the vet's like those bags of old stuff no one wants any more you see dumped outside charity shops. She thought it would be easier for us all that way, she said. Less upsetting. You've got to wonder sometimes what planet she's on.

Where was Tilly's body now? What happened to all the bodies? What did the vet do with them? I couldn't bear to think about it.

I thought, at least if Tilly had had a grave, I could put some flowers on it and make it lovely. That was supposed to make you feel better. So I got a jam jar, filled it with water and picked some nasturtiums from Tilly's favourite digging spot in the flowerbed under the window.

I took it to the potting shed and cleared a space for it on the window ledge. Then I went to my room to get the photo I had of Tilly in that miniature frame you got in your Christmas cracker, the one you swapped for the tiny tape measure I got in mine. I picked up her squeaky toy from the butterfly patch on my way back to the potting shed.

Of all the rings and balls and rubber animals she'd had in a lifetime of toys, why was it an old rubber sandwich with yellow cheese and blue lettuce in the middle that she loved the best?

I put the photo and the squeaky sandwich beside the flowers and sat down on the chewed-up cushions. I tried to tell myself I felt better, but I didn't really. In fact, going out there to sit with Tilly seemed to make me feel even more sad.

So I took her photo back to my room and copied it on a big sheet of paper. Then I started painting. Laying the colours on top of each other – brown, grey, white, black – was almost like stroking Tilly's fur, and it made me feel calmer. I was painting her eyes when you came in.

'That's really good,' you said. 'It looks just like her.'

I touched each dark grey eye with a drop of white, and they lit up.

'I wish I could paint,' you sighed.

You leant against the wall, still looking at my picture.

'I suppose she was quite old. And if she was sick, like the vet said… Well, it probably was the kindest thing.'

So that was how they had dressed it up for you. How they had made it seem okay.

'It's still hard, though,' you said. 'She was part of the family, wasn't she?'

I wondered if that was why you had come to my room, to talk about Tilly, and see if I was all right. You hadn't done that sort of thing before, so maybe in some strange way, the party had started to bring us closer. I suppose you did still think I'd organised it all for you.

I wished I could really talk to you but if I did, I would have to start by coming clean about that, and then I would have to say, 'I flushed your tablets down the toilet and I think I've got to tell Mum. You shouldn't have made me promise to keep a secret like that.'

I'd have to tell you, 'Tilly wasn't sick – they murdered her because of your lumps.' Which wouldn't be fair because it wasn't your fault; you never asked them to do it.

It was good to feel that some time in the future we might actually take to talking more but right now, the way things were, you hanging around was only stirring me up again.

I wanted you to go, so I could get on with my painting. I'd drawn the jam jar full of nasturtiums on one side of Tilly and her squeaky cheese sandwich on the other, so there was still a lot to do.

You went over to the window.

'Are you still going out with Tris? Only I think you should be careful.'

You left a pause for me to ask why but when I didn't, you told me anyway.

'He's not a nice guy. He sleeps around and boasts about it.'

I didn't believe you but anyway, even if Tris had slept around, that might just have been because he had'nt met the right person.

'Steer clear of him, yeah?' you said.

Then I really wanted you to go because I thought you were sticking your nose in. Tris had got tickets for Shakespeare in the Park on the Saturday, for our first proper date on our own together, which was really romantic, and I wasn't going to let what you said spoil it for me. It was the one thing I was really looking forward to.

I hadn't told Mum and Dad I was going out because I wasn't talking to them and I didn't see why I should

JENNY ALEXANDER

have to tell them. When the day came, I just went.

Tris was waiting for me at the ice-cream kiosk by the East Gate of the park. He was wearing a slightly crumpled cream linen jacket and he looked about twenty-five. We got some coffees and sat down at one of the tables because we had half an hour to kill before the play began. You could see the seating scaffold they had erected for the performance on the grass beyond the lake.

I asked him stuff like which university he was going to and what he wanted to do after that. 'Way to make small talk,' Lexi would have said, but I'd say, 'Way to get to know someone.'

I noticed he didn't say 'I'd like to go to the Birmingham School of Acting', or 'I'm hoping to be an actor'. He said, 'I'm going to the Birmingham School of Acting; I'm going to be an actor'. He was so full of self-confidence. 'A real go-getter' Nan would say.

He asked me what I was going to do with my life and I said I wanted to be an artist, though I felt silly saying it because I didn't really think I'd be good enough, and everyone was expecting me to go to university and be a teacher or something instead.

Tris said we were soulmates; he'd expect to get an invitation to my first exhibition and he'd definitely send me front row tickets for his West-End debut. I saw our future stretching out ahead of us like a red carpet, bright and exciting.

82

Since we were soulmates, I considered telling him about what Mum and Dad had done to Tilly. If I did, maybe I would cry, and he would put his arms around me and then he would hold me until it all felt better.

But on the other hand, he might get embarrassed and be cross with me for blubbing, and never ask me out again. I decided not to say anything, because even soulmates should probably tread carefully in the early stages.

'Time to go if we want to get good seats,' he said, standing up.

It was starting to spit as we walked across the grass, but at least the air was warm. Some people in the queue had brought umbrellas, in case the weather turned.

The play was *King Lear* – you know, the one where the old king gives his kingdom to his daughters and then they throw him out in the cold because he hasn't got any power over them any more. Well, maybe you don't know, since you've never been that keen on going to the theatre.

There's this bit towards the end where Lear goes crazy and starts wandering about in the night, stark naked and barking mad. You don't expect it to literally happen on stage but that night the actor actually took all his clothes off, so there really was this starkers old man, right there in front of us, pacing up and down, muttering and gibbering.

It was nearly dark by then, and starting to get cold, and you could see a mist of rain in the single spotlight that followed the old king. He shook his fists and shouted at the sky to rain and hail on him when, all of a sudden, there was this massive crack of thunder and the rain really did come bucketing down.

The actors kept on going, shouting above the storm, and the audience totally went with it. Nobody moved. Nobody put up their umbrellas or fumbled with their coats. We craned forward, trying to hear above the drumming of the rain, blinking the rainwater from our eyes.

By the time the performance had finished everyone was shivering and soaked to the skin, but happy because something magical had happened. Then the lights went up and the magic was broken. There was a scrum for the exit, with people rushing to get back home in the warm. Tris and me were splashing back across the park when he suddenly stopped and pulled me towards him.

His mouth was warm, as I tasted his lips, his teeth, his tongue, but our faces were cold, and the water from my wet hair was trickling down my back. Our clothes stuck hard to our bodies in the dark.

I hadn't been out with anyone since Jason Crane, and that had been different. Neither of us had really had a clue, I could see that now, but Tris knew what he was doing.

'Have you ever stripped off naked in the rain?'

I laughed.

'No, really,' he goes. 'It must be a great feeling.'

We were near the Peace Garden by then, and he nodded towards the entrance. 'Why don't we go in there and give it a try? There's no one about.'

I shouted above the rain that I was too cold, but he tugged at my arm, as if he couldn't hear. I pulled away. The whole evening had been perfect and amazing. Why did he have to go and spoil it? I started walking on, feeling angry with him and upset with myself. He caught up with me, laughing, as if it had all been a joke.

By the time we got back to the house, I'd convinced myself he probably had just been joking. I mean, who seriously goes running around in the rain with all their clothes off in a public park, unless of course they were playing King Lear?

I was the one who had spoiled everything. I'd been in an angry mood for days because of Tilly, and it had been easy to slip into being angry with him.

So I was already feeling bad when I went inside, and the last thing I needed was Mum pouncing on me saying 'Look at the state of you!' and 'Where on earth have you been?'

I ignored her, but she kept on nagging me all the way up the stairs.

'You're supposed to tell us when you're going out...' etc, etc.

I went straight to the bathroom to get a towel, but she stopped me from shutting the door. I crossed my arms.

'What?'

'We've been worried sick.'

'And?'

'Jessie, we're not cross. We're just trying to look out for you.'

'Like you looked out for Tilly?'

She took a step back then, and I shut the door.

I sent Tris a text to say what a great night it had been but he didn't text me back. I was fed up with myself for over-reacting, when he'd just been larking around. And even if he hadn't... well, so what?

I mean, he was right – taking your clothes off in the pouring rain must be a fantastic feeling. The water on your bare skin; in your hair, your mouth, your eyes. Plus, of course, it was dark in the Peace Garden, and my body would have looked all sleek and gleaming. If he was the one, then I was bound to be getting my clothes off with him soon, and it would be much less embarrassing in the dark.

I thought I could fall in love with Tris because he looked so perfect and I fancied him like mad and he said we were soulmates, and if I fell in love with him I'd want to go all the way with him, which had, of course, been the plan all along. So did it really matter if things happened in the wrong order, and I had sex with him first and then fell in love?

Some girls had sex with boys on the first date, but they were slappers. Were you still a slapper if you slept with someone you hardly knew, if you were planning to fall in love?

I texted him again. Of course, it might just be that he was too busy to text me back now that his exams had started. I said, *Good luck with your exams – you don't need it! xxx*.

In between wondering why Tris wasn't texting me, I worked on my painting. I dressed all in black, like people used to in the old days when they went into proper mourning, and got a piece of black cloth from my scraps bag to cover my desk, so the picture was framed in black as I worked.

Tilly was finished now, and she looked just right. You can't get a painting to look like a photograph – well I can't anyway – but why would you want to? Tilly wasn't a photograph; she was a living creature.

Most of the background was still just sketched in, so it looked like Tilly was sitting in a drawing, not part of a whole scene. Filling in the pencil lines with colour would bring the whole picture to life. I started with the nasturtiums, putting the jar on the black cloth in front of me, and really taking my time to look at the flowers.

Lexi sent me this quote once, from Albert Einstein, which said there are only two ways to live your life – one as though nothing is a miracle, and the other as though everything is a miracle. But I think that when you really look at things, there is only one way.

Life and death are there in a jar of nasturtiums, some shrivelling up, some still waiting to unfold and in the middle, wide open among their round, starry leaves, the fresh, full flowers in their moment of glory. Flame red, bright orange, deep yellow, their papery petals pale where the light shines through them, and dark where they overlap.

A person needs loud music when they're painting orange. Dad came in to make me turn it down but as soon as he'd gone, I turned it up again. Mum stuck her head round the door like she always does when I'm painting – she thinks art's just an excuse for not doing something useful, such as homework or tidying my room. She tutted, I glared, she left. I knew I'd have to forgive them in the end, but I wasn't ready to do it yet.

Nan came over on the Wednesday evening. She sat out in the garden with Mum for a while, before coming to look for me. I was working on Tilly's squeaky toy by then, which was hard because it was covered in chew marks and little holes where she'd managed to bite through. Nobody had washed it or anything, so it must still have had her saliva on it – a real physical trace of Tilly, when all the rest of her had gone.

'That's so good,' Nan said. 'You've really captured her.'

'Thanks,' I muttered, not looking up.

'Are you angry with me for telling you not to worry?'

I dipped my brush in the water and swirled it round.

'I thought there wasn't any point in you worrying, because, in the end, it was never going to be your decision. I offered to look after Tilly myself, but it wasn't my decision either. It was up to your parents, and they did what they thought was right.'

'So murder is right?'

'It wasn't easy for them. They loved Tilly, too.'

'They had a funny way of showing it.'

'Well, I suppose I'd better let you get on...'

It's difficult painting white things because they can come out milky-looking. You have to keep the colours pure and sharp. The key is in the details, such as the dark holes where Tilly's teeth had gone in. The yellow cheese in the middle was easier, with its etching of shadow, and then the lettuce, which the sun had bleached from green to blue.

When I had finished the squeaky sandwich I had to paint in behind it, setting it firmly in the grass beside Tilly and her flowers. Each blade of grass grew smoothly under the brush, so soothing, so necessary.

As I worked, I could hear Marky kicking the football against the side wall. He seemed to be doing a lot more of that lately. Maybe football did the same for him as painting did for me. It couldn't make the bad things go away, but it kind of moved you into a different space until you could bear to face up to them.

At some point, the steady thud of the football stopped, and Marky came indoors for a bit. When he saw my picture, he said 'Wow!' and 'That's so cool!' and 'Can you do one for me?' I told him I would lend him my paints and he could do one for himself.

'It's better that way,' I said. 'Then it's your picture.'

Lexi says some people can paint and some people can't, but that's not what I think. Everyone can make a mark on the paper – it's down to how you interpret the mark. The difference between artists and people who don't paint is that artists love the marks they make.

Sometimes, when I stopped to change the music, I noticed my phone hadn't rung, and then I wondered if I'd blown it with Tris, by just being too young. Driving out to a country pub, seeing Shakespeare in the park – they weren't exactly the kinds of date I was used to. Maybe Mum was right about him; maybe he was too old for me.

But that idea never lasted long. It dissolved in the colours like every other thought that happened to drop into my head. And finally, there was nothing left to finish but the sky.

I made it cloudless and clear, almost white on one side of Tilly's head and shoulders, becoming darker as I moved across, so that the bright nasturtiums floated up into a sea of blue.

I've just read back over that last bit, Seb, and I don't know why I banged on about painting so much. I mean, I know it isn't your thing. I think I was maybe putting off telling you what happened next with Tris, because that isn't going to be easy. I'm going to do it now. I'm going to keep writing now until it's done.

So anyway, for ages after our date in the park nothing much actually happened at all, except I kept texting Tris and he kept ignoring me. I didn't know which days he had exams or how many he was taking, but I guessed he was spending every spare minute revising, which I was too, as soon as my study leave began.

I just wished he would text me something, so that I would know whether we were still seeing each other or not, and the more I didn't hear from him, the more I wanted to.

I was walking home after my second German exam when he finally messaged me. He thanked me for sending him all those texts, and apologised for not answering, but it was a weird time, he said, and he hadn't been thinking about anything but exams.

I texted straight back and told him that was okay, I completely understood, what with doing exams too, and were we still going out?

Tris said sure, if I wanted to, and it would be really great if I came to his end of exams celebration party. GCSEs hadn't actually finished yet but I said yes anyway, because it might be our last chance to see each other before he and his family went on holiday.

This time I told Mum and Dad I was going. I didn't ask – I just said. Since the stormy night, it wasn't only me who was angry with them – they were angry with me too, so I didn't want to push it.

Mum gave me a grilling. 'Who's going to be there? Will Lexi be invited?' For the first time ever, it seemed like Lexi being invited would actually be a good thing.

Lexi said she and Monk would pick me up on the way, and bring me home afterwards if I wanted. I was hoping Tris would walk me home again, and it might actually be raining, because if he said let's get naked again this time I might not chicken out, but I knew he probably wouldn't be able to leave his own party.

I got ready early, which was stupid because it meant I had plenty of time to start losing my nerve. Now we knew his address, it turned out that he didn't live in a big house on the hill like I'd imagined, but in one of those boring new semis behind Tesco Metro, so I had to adjust my mental image of Tris at home.

No swimming pool, no grand high-ceilinged rooms, no spectacular views of the park but, instead, a small tidy garden, a beige living room and the hard dazzle of sunlight on the cars in Tesco's car park. The villa in Sardinia was probably a time-share; I had to adjust my idea of that too.

It was weird, but knowing Tris wasn't really rich didn't put me off him at all. In fact, it made me like him even better, because it showed what a great actor he was, being able to make people believe he was born with a silver spoon in his mouth when he wasn't.

I liked that we had even more in common than I'd thought. He probably did get his lovely clothes in the Oxfam shop like me and have nine-to-five type parents who didn't understand his dreams.

While I was waiting for Lexi and Monk, I lay down on my bed and thought about Tris. It was sad he was going away for a whole month on Monday, but maybe that could actually be a good thing.

We would chat online and send each other emails, which would be a great chance for us to get to know each other better. When we knew each other better we would almost certainly fall properly in love. Absence makes the heart grow fonder – everyone knows that.

By the time the doorbell rang, it was after ten o'clock, so there was no way Mum and Dad could still expect me to be home by midnight. I ran downstairs to answer it, sticking my head round the living room door on my way out.

'Monk's giving me a lift back. Don't wait up,' I said.

Tris's driveway was crammed with cars so we had to park round the corner, but we could hear the party as soon as we got out of the car.

The front door was wide open, and some girl I didn't know was throwing up in the flowerbed outside. We had to push our way past two couples eating each other's faces on the step.

Inside, the hallway was heaving with sweaty people and the music pouring out of the room on the right was so loud you could feel the floor and walls vibrating. The only light seemed to be coming from the kitchen up ahead.

We fought our way through to get some drinks, but it was too noisy to have a three-way conversation, so I left Lexi and Monk and went looking for Tris. I recognised some of the faces – it seemed like most of the Year 13s were there, as well as a few Year 12s. But there were tons of other people who looked older. Where had they all come from?

I thought I saw Tris by the French windows, but when he turned round I realised it wasn't him. It was someone older, who looked just like him – a big brother? I hadn't asked him about his family at all. There were so many things I didn't know about him yet, and I couldn't wait to find out.

I felt a hand on my shoulder.

'Hi, Jess.' He kissed my neck.

Tris didn't introduce me to people but if anyone asked he just said 'This is Jess'; he didn't add 'We're seeing each other' or anything. We danced and from time to time, he pushed his way through to the kitchen to get us some more drinks.

He was just drinking coke, because he wanted to stay sober in case the party got out of hand, but I had vodka with mine to numb my nerves. Every time my glass was empty, Tris filled it up again straight away. He was so attentive and lovely. The funny thing was that the more I drank, the stronger it tasted.

Everything was going fine until I suddenly needed a pee. The room had been swaying a bit, but as I went out into the hall, the whole house suddenly listed like a ship and I seriously thought I was going to be sick. I saw the bottom stair lurch up at me, and kind of half fell and half sat down on it.

I don't know how long I was there before I remembered I needed the loo, but when I stood up again my head was spinning so much I had to lean against the wall. I'd seen lots of people off their faces before – like the girl at our party who pissed in her jeans – but it had never happened to me.

Tris appeared – or had he been there all the time? He pulled me to my feet and helped me up the stairs. There were people in all the upstairs rooms; Lexi and Monk were probably among them. I tried to go into the bathroom by myself, but missed the door and crashed into the frame. Tris had to help me through.

When I'd finished, I couldn't get the bathroom door open, so it was just as well I hadn't managed to lock it. Tris heard me fumbling around and let me out.

'I'd better take you home,' he said.

The stairs were moving like a ribbon on a breeze, and I don't know how we managed to get to the bottom. I wanted Lexi to come and stop me, to be like Mum and tell me 'You're not going anywhere in that state, young lady! You're staying here with me!' But I didn't see Lexi, and the next thing I knew, the cold air hit me like a wave and knocked me clean off my feet.

Tris lay me down on the back seat, probably because I couldn't sit up. I shut my eyes. The seat felt rough against my cheek, vibrating softly to the rhythm of the engine. We seemed to be taking some wrong turnings, but I couldn't even open my eyes, let alone find the words to tell Tris.

I must have dozed off, because the car stopping woke me up. It was very dark. Why weren't the streetlights on? Was there a power cut in our road? Tris opened the door and I could see a high hedge behind him. Where were the houses?

He sat me up and got into the back of the car beside me. He put one arm around me and, tipping my face towards him, kissed my lips quite softly. I realised he was fumbling with my jeans. He pulled them down, and one leg came out. It fell towards the floor like something that wasn't connected to me at all.

'What are you doing?' I said, or I think I said it, but I'm not sure, because Tris didn't seem to hear.

He shoved his hand inside my knickers, then pulled them down as well. He undid his own trousers and pressed himself against me again, kissing me so hard I couldn't breathe, pushing his tongue right into my mouth.

This wasn't the way it was supposed to be. It wasn't the way I had imagined. When we finally made love, he was supposed to gaze into my eyes, until I turned my face slightly and he dipped down to my neck, and we both closed our eyes in ecstasy.

We were supposed to feel like swimmers cleaving through the waves, lifting and dipping as the waves got bigger and bigger, until we finally collapsed into each other, full of gratitude and love.

In the back of Tris's car it wasn't anything like that. It reminded me, more than anything else, of when a randy dog gets hold of your leg and rubs itself up and down, until you shake it off. But he was hurting me, and I couldn't shake him off, and I couldn't cry out because of his mouth pressing down so hard over mine.

It was over really suddenly. I thought I was going to be sick. I felt dizzy, and really confused. What just happened? How did that happen? Why was Tris behaving as if it hadn't happened at all?

'I'll call you, yeah?' he said, when he got me home.

I was sobering up by then, but I wished I wasn't. I felt as if I was waking up from a really upsetting dream that I couldn't fully remember. It seemed surprising, somehow, that I wasn't crying.

The clock on the dashboard said quarter past one. The lights were on in the house. The concrete path was still and solid, and the world wasn't moving any more.

'Did the earth move for you?' they say. The earth was moving like crazy, I thought, right up to the moment that me and Tris got it on. Then it stopped. The earth stopped moving for me.

That was ironic, I thought. I wanted to tell someone. Oddly enough, the person I wanted to tell was you, Seb. But you were already in bed.

The next thing I knew, I was lying under my duvet in the dark. I seemed to remember Mum, when I got home, saying 'Christ!' and 'What time do you call this?' and 'How much have you had to drink?' but I couldn't remember her actually being there, it was just words.

My head was full of words, and some of them had pictures attached. A leg falling to the floor. An open belt buckle. Headlights sweeping through the inside of a car.

Words said: 'I'm not a virgin any more.'

Weren't you supposed to feel different in some way, like before you were a girl, and now you were a woman? His hand inside my knickers.

Reassuring words: 'I was drunk so it wasn't my fault.'

Harsh words: 'I knew I was getting drunk and I could have stopped.'

Confusing words: 'Maybe I secretly wanted it to happen.'

It was confusing because I knew that I did want it to happen, only not like that, and not right then, so perhaps I just wasn't clear enough and Tris got confused too.

Did this mean that he and I had a relationship now? Would I be doing it with him again, when I was sober? At least I wouldn't have to think about that for a while, what with him going off to Sardinia.

Sardinia. Sparkling seas. A ship with white sails. Me in a long red dress, floating out on the breeze. The night turned into a choppy crossing towards the far-off shores of morning, punctuated by bits of dream and bouts of churning seasickness.

When the sunlight woke me up, I was expecting to have a massive hangover, so I put off seeing whether I could get out of bed. My head felt dull and fuzzy. I didn't feel particularly sick, but as I put my dressing gown on and dragged myself downstairs it was as if gravity had got stronger, so every movement was a massive effort.

I didn't want to see anyone but I was desperate for a glass of water, so I had to go into the kitchen. Mum was making lunch. She took one look at me and launched into her dangers-of-drinking-too-much lecture.

I let it go over my head. At least if she was banging on about alcohol she wasn't examining me for evidence of sex. I felt sure it must show that I had done it with Tris, and she would notice straight away if she bothered to look.

Mum cracked a raw egg into the blender and my stomach lurched. She added some milk and a spoonful of honey, poured it into a glass and told me to drink it. An excess of alcohol was a dreadful assault on your system, she said. 'You need a proper pick-me-up full of nutrients to help your body recover.'

She stood over me while I glopped it down. I only managed it by concentrating on not thinking about the raw egg and pretending it was a honey-flavoured smoothie. But the minute I'd finished, the raw egg came wobbling into my brain and I had to run straight upstairs and stick my head down the loo.

I wasn't going back down any time soon, so I opened my computer and went online to see if Lexi was around. She wasn't, but she had sent me a picture of Doris with five tiny puppies. They weren't so much cute-and-cuddly as bald-and-slug-like, and Doris didn't seem to be that taken with them.

The message said: *Doris is proud to announce the*

safe arrival of Zac, Paulie, Momo, Prin and Digger.

I heard the blip that meant Lexi had come online. She didn't say anything about the party because it was all puppies, puppies, puppies. Doris had just had the first one when she got home, and Lexi and her mum had sat up into the small hours of the morning while she delivered the rest.

You've got to come round and see them, she messaged.

Lexi was unusually gushy about the whole puppy thing, and when she finally got round to talking about Monk it seemed like some of the gushiness had spilt over.

He's the most interesting person I've ever met. He's so intelligent and adventurous, plus he's a great kisser. I think I'm in love!

I wasn't sure I liked this new Lexi. Probably, I was just jealous of her, though.

Then she wrote: *I'm wondering if I should sleep with him. Do you think I should?*

The first thing I thought was, They haven't done it yet! The second thing I thought was, Why is she asking me?

How should I know? I wrote.

Well, you slept with Tris.

Who says?

Tris does. He texted his mates and someone told Monk.

What, so Monk had to tell you too?

Well it isn't exactly a secret.

I sat there staring at the screen. I knew I should say something back, but I couldn't seem to take it in. I looked at the words until they were starting to do my head in, then pushed back my chair and went to the bathroom to splash some cold water on my face.

When I came back, new messages were blipping through from Lexi all the time: *Are you still there? Where have you gone? Sorry, I thought you knew. He said it was amazing...*

I closed the door behind me and leant against it, wondering how my life had gone from okay to terrible in such a short time, when a tap on the door nearly made me jump out of my skin.

'Jess?' you said softly. 'Are you all right?'

I moved away from the door.

'Mum said you got really drunk last night. Were you at Tris's party?'

Nearly everyone in the sixth form was at the party but he hadn't invited you, not that you were bothered, considering you didn't like parties and you didn't like Tris either.

A new message blipped in from Lexi, and we both looked at the laptop lying open on my bed.

He didn't say your name. He said: Sex with a girl with blue hair. Amazing!

You saw all the messages.

You said: 'Are you okay?'

I shrugged.

'He seemed so… so perfect.'

I knew you wouldn't say 'I told you so'.

All you knew was that he'd texted his mates, which was bad enough, but you probably thought the sex was like he said, amazing. The flickering pictures flashed through my head – the leg falling down, the buckle, the headlights. I wanted to tell you what it had really been like, but in the cold light of day it just felt too hard.

You told me not to worry. It would all blow over.

'Everyone knows what a knob he is – they'll think nothing really happened and he was lying to make himself look big.'

I said, 'What if he took pictures?'

You sat down on the bed.

'So he wasn't lying then?'

I shook my head, and sat down beside you.

You said, 'If he had pictures, he'd have sent one of those to his mates instead. He hasn't, Jess. So don't worry.'

I must have still looked worried, because you went on trying to make me feel better.

'Whatever Tris does isn't any reflection on you. It just shows what a low-life he is.'

I wanted you to stay and keep talking, even though nothing you said could make it better. Just having you there felt like something. Something I could hold on to.

'Thank you for coming to check on me,' I said.

We were so awkward together. We'd only started talking to each other about things that mattered since your party, and that was all built on a lie.

'So, you are going to be all right?' you said, in the voice of a person who was about to go.

'Were you at Della's last night?' I asked, to keep you there a little longer.

You nodded.

'Lexi says Della's lucky you keep taking her back because you're out of her league.'

You frowned, as if you had never thought about leagues and stuff.

'What league are you in when you've got a missing foot?'

I hadn't realised you even thought about your foot any more because, I suppose, I didn't. But when you said it, I could see how stupid that was, because though we hardly ever saw your stump, it was the first thing you would see every morning, and the last thing every night.

Of course it would bother you, but I hadn't known, and there must be lots of other things I didn't know. I wished you would talk to me some more, but I didn't know how to keep the conversation going.

'D'you want some tea and toast?' you said.

You went to get some for me, while I sat on the bed, waiting. You had never brought me breakfast before and it was nice, but strange. I thought your strangeness was about the bad thing that had happened to me, but I can see now that it was also about the bad thing that was about to happen to you.

I was glad you made enough toast for yourself too, and stayed to eat it with me. You said you were going to clear out your room that afternoon. I asked why, considering it was already the tidiest room in the house. 'I'm sorting out the stuff I won't need when I go to university.'

You said things like 'I'm just across the hall' and 'come and have a chat if you want to' and when I didn't, you kept looking in on me to see if I wanted more tea or something else to eat.

If you hadn't noticed the sleeping pills were gone before, you certainly would now, and every time you came in, I braced myself for an argument. But as the afternoon wore on and you still didn't say anything, I thought perhaps you'd known for ages but it didn't matter that much. It really had been just a comfort thing, like you said, and you didn't need it any more.

At the end of the afternoon, you came into my room with a piece of paper. You had written a list of your possessions, which started, 'For Jess...' I read it.

'Your thinking chair?'

You knew how much I coveted that bashed-up leather armchair you got from Nan when Grampy died.

'I won't need it at university.'

'Yes, but your laptop too? You're going to need that.'

'I'm getting a new one.'

'This is silly,' I said. 'You're not going for ages.' I put the list back in your hand.

You said you and Della had tickets for a lecture at the Science Museum that evening, and you'd be staying over at her house afterwards.

'You will be all right, won't you?'

I nodded. You dropped your list on my dressing table on your way out. I hadn't thought much until then about you going away to university, but now it suddenly hit me.

All my life, from the day I was born, even after your cancer when we stopped being close, you had always been there, and without you everything would feel completely different.

I realised I was going to miss you very much.

You had already left for the lecture so it was only me and Marky at suppertime. I'd been avoiding Mum all day, but I got a full blast of the dangers of drinking and, nearly as bad, Dad examining my face and telling me that, actually, I did look awful.

I wanted to go to bed, sleep for a couple of months and wake up a different person in a different life. But when I crawled under the duvet at nine o'clock, I couldn't get to sleep.

Every part of my body hurt, as if I had fallen into

some massive machine and been pummelled half to death. I couldn't stop thinking about what had happened with Tris, but my thoughts were broken into bits and refused to come together into something I could understand.

I wished you hadn't gone to Della's again. It would have felt better knowing you were just across the hall. I wished I had been able to talk to you about Tris. I mean, you knew him. You knew he was a knob. You didn't judge me. You asked me if I was all right.

What if I was pregnant? After all Mum's safe sex talks, it wasn't as if I could tell myself that wasn't possible the first time. How could I have been so stupid and, if I was pregnant, how could I tell Mum and Dad?

I thought maybe you could do it for me, like you did when it came to asking if we could have a party, because you were Mum's favourite and Dad always went along with Mum when it came to you, and that meant you could say nothing wrong.

Or maybe we wouldn't have to tell them about the baby if I got a termination, but that was just a fancy word for killing your baby, and I didn't think I could do it. Even if I could, I had no idea how you went about it.

I remembered when I was six or seven, I used to trail around after you, my brilliant big brother. You taught me how to ride my bike and helped me learn my tables; you knew things, because you were older.

Back then, we had been really close, but when someone gets ill, they kind of disappear. People see the illness first, and not the person behind it. That's what happened to you Seb; you disappeared.

After all those years of missing you, I felt like I was finally finding you again, at the very moment when you were just about to leave. That made me feel so sad – because it was too late.

But then I thought, maybe it wasn't too late. Maybe when you weren't at home any more you could come out from behind the illness at last and, far away from Mum and Dad and me and Marky, become a completely new person with no history, who just happened to have a false foot.

And then when we saw each other out there in the world, we could be a proper big brother and little sister again, and if I was pregnant and didn't get an abortion, even if Mum and Dad went mental and I ended up in a grotty bedsit like Lexi's brother's ex-girlfriend and their baby, Bo, at least I would have you, and you would be a lovely uncle to my baby. Uncle Seb.

I must have dozed off for a couple of hours, because the birds woke me up when it was just beginning to get light. I felt like crap. I put my dressing gown on and went downstairs.

If Tilly had still been alive, I would have sat on the floor beside her basket, and stroked her head. She would have rested her chin on my leg. The warmth of her small body would have made everything feel better. An animal can do that. They remind you what's important, which in the end comes down to breathing in and breathing out.

Someone had left the garden blankets beside the back door. I picked them up, and a sprinkle of dried-up grass cuttings fell on the floor. I decided to go to the potting shed, which was the nearest thing Tilly had to a grave, now that I'd put the squeaky sandwich back out there on one side of her photo and the jar of flowers on the other.

Outside, the air was cool, and the grass was wet under my bare feet. The fruit trees were full of cobwebs, bright and shiny with dew. Everything was misty pale except for the apples on the farthest tree, which were as big as ping-pong balls and already red, though it would be a while before they would be sweet enough to eat.

The potting shed door was stuck. I pushed harder against it. There seemed to be something blocking it inside. Suddenly, I remembered the night of our party, when the voice in the potting shed had said, 'Piss off'. I put my shoulder to the door and managed to get it open enough to be able to squeeze inside. It closed itself behind me.

I saw you, of course I did, but I couldn't look. I stared at the gin bottle that had rolled into the corner. The first thing I thought was that you were drunk. That's what I tried to think, anyway.

One of Nan's brown plastic tablet bottles was lying on the floor beside your hand. There were still a few tablets in it. You must have discovered I'd got rid of the first lot, and simply gone back to steal some more.

You were lying on your back with your arms slightly out from your sides, and your head resting on one of the old chewed-up cushions. Your eyes were almost closed, and you had this little smile on your face, as if you knew something that no one else knew. It was a lovely, lazy smile. I couldn't remember ever seeing you like that before.

I fell to my knees beside you wanting to wake you up, but when I touched your arm it was cold and stiff. My stomach lurched and I pulled away. I heard this horrible groaning noise, really loud and close by, like an animal in pain, and I didn't realise straight away that it was coming from me.

Your body was a waxwork now; I knew you were no longer inside it. I leaned my head forward, really slowly, until my face was so close to your chest that I could smell the damp cloth of your coat.

I wasn't me and you weren't you; there was nothing in that space except the terrible groaning, which seemed to come out of the walls and the roof and the cracked concrete floor. It went on and on until I pressed my face hard into your cold coat and rocked back and forth, as if you were rocking me.

When the rocking stopped, there was this eerie

stillness. No flow of breath, no beating heart where your beating heart should be. You were not in your body any more... yet you were here. I could feel you.

I sat up, slowly pulling the blankets around me, my eyes on your body but my heart feeling your spirit so close by. It was as if you had dissolved into the air, like an invisible cloud, hovering around me.

If I opened the door, you would be sucked away from me for ever, so we hung in there together, the two of us – just you and me in the cold white dawn.

Moment by moment, the daylight started bringing the colours to life. The ivy on the damp wall lit up in all its greens. Tilly's flowers made their daytime splash of orange against the window. I wondered whether you had noticed Tilly looking down on you while you were shovelling Nan's sleeping pills down your throat.

This was my fault. I'd known about the tablets, and I hadn't done enough about it. I'd kept it to myself and not told anyone, like I'd promised. My body was numb and rigid with cold; I wasn't even shivering any more. I put my forehead on my knees, and closed my eyes.

A thousand years later, someone called my name from the other side of the universe, and the thin distant sound pulled me back. They must have been in my room and seen I wasn't there, and now they were looking for me.

That's when I realised how cunning you had been.

Nobody had known you were missing because you had told us all that you were staying the night at Della's. You must have hidden the gin and pills in the potting shed before you went to the lecture, then crept round the back of the house when you got home. If you actually went to the lecture at all.

You had lied so that no one would start looking for you until the next day, and then it would be too late to cart you off unconscious and pump you out again. But you knew we would find you in the end, because you were there all the time, right under our noses.

Dad pushed the door. He peered in through the window. Then all hell broke loose. What could I do? I moved away from the door and they came in; I don't know where you went after that.

There was so much screaming and shouting. Mum was saying we had to get an ambulance, and Dad was saying, 'What's the point? Can't you see that he's dead?'

Mum was shaking your body as if it was still you, and Dad was frantically questioning me. 'How long have you been here? Why didn't you call us?'

Mum stopped shaking you. 'If we call an ambulance, they'll take him away,' she said, in this weird voice, as if she was talking to herself.

I went and sat on the decking outside the annexe. Things happened. The police; the ambulance. They asked me stupid things like 'Did your brother leave a letter?' and 'Did he say anything to you that might suggest he was thinking of taking his own life?'

It wasn't that I wanted to be difficult, it was just that my voice seemed to have gone. I was dumb like you are in a dream when the axe-man is creeping up on you and you can't cry out; you don't even open your mouth because you know that no sound will come.

Marigold said I should write about how I felt. Well, that's how I felt, like it was all happening in a dream, and soon I would wake up. Or like I was watching a frightening film; it wasn't real, and it wasn't really happening to me.

Marigold said that writing it down would unlock things for me, and I thought she meant it would make all this start to feel real, but do you know what, Seb? I've written it down now and it still feels just the same.

THREE

'Did you write anything this week?' Marigold said.

I nodded.

'Did you write about finding your brother's body?'

I nodded again.

I had remembered to bring her gel pens back, and they were lying on the low square table beside us. Marigold's pens this week were brown and blue. How did she decide which colours to bring?

All the stuff that I had written was in a padded envelope in my school bag. Normally, I would never have taken anything like that to school, in case someone found it and took the piss. But I was like a ghost since I'd stopped talking. Hardly anyone even noticed I was there, so who would care what I had in my bag?

Marigold said, 'I know you've written it to Sebastian, and it's private between you two, but you can always show it to me if you would like me to read it too.'

I did want her to read it, and it would have been so easy just to open my bag, take out the envelope and pass it across to her. I could have done it without speaking. It was what I had planned to do. I managed to shake my head.

'That's okay, Jess,' she said. 'You mustn't feel you have to share anything you don't want to.'

I sat there looking down, fed up with myself for bottling it. I started to notice things again – the stain on the carpet, and the silver trim on Marigold's shoes; the clock slicing up the time into tiny tick-tock pieces; the air moving in and out of me like the sea.

'Did you tell Seb how you felt when you found him?' Marigold said.

I nodded again.

'I'm glad you can nod your head for me now,' she smiled. 'It makes me feel that we're really making a connection.'

We sat in silence for a while. Marigold really didn't seem to mind that I hadn't shown her what I had written, or even that I still wasn't talking, so perhaps it was okay. I started to relax. These sessions had become important; they had become the only important thing, and I didn't want Marigold to think they were a waste of time.

Writing to you had been a good idea. It had meant that you and me had, as Marigold would say, a connection. Also, it had given me something to do, to fill the endless emptiness you left behind.

But it hadn't got me talking like it was supposed to, and now the silence, which used to feel like being inside a safe and see-through plastic box, had turned into a prison.

Marigold had to help me. She had to get me out.

'Give me another task,' I thought. 'Tell me what to do.'

Marigold said, 'Losing someone we love is probably the hardest thing we ever have to deal with. There are so many difficult emotions; we can feel overwhelmed.'

She said a bereaved person could have so much sadness, they might feel that they couldn't go on. She told me family members of people who commit suicide are nine times more likely than other people to do it themselves.

Marigold stopped talking. She seemed to be examining me for signs of sadness. I could feel her eyes on me even though I was looking at the floor. It's just amazing how much you never notice normally, I thought. The dust along the top of the electric sockets, the dead spider under the chair.

Marigold said, 'It's all right to cry.'

After a while, when I still hadn't cried, Marigold started talking again. She said that the normal sadness of bereavement was worse when someone had committed suicide; as well as being sad for them because they'd died, you also felt sad that they were unhappy enough to want to do it.

This was a distortion, she said. It was the same distortion that went on in the person's mind when they decided to kill themselves. At that moment, maybe it seemed like a good idea, because at that moment they felt so unhappy. But it was just a moment in a lifetime of moments, some good, some bad.

Marigold said we shouldn't assume that your life had been unusually unhappy, just that you'd had an unusually unhappy moment. Lots of people toyed with the idea of killing themselves, she said, and some even made plans and preparations, but not so many people experienced a moment of such intensity that they could actually see it through.

Marigold said it was important to remember the good times, because that would help me to cope with my own sadness. If I'd been talking, maybe I would have told Marigold that I didn't feel particularly sad. I didn't seem to feel particularly anything, except numb and kind of spacey.

But maybe I wouldn't tell her that, because then she might think I was some kind of heartless freak, which, when I came to think about it, I supposed must be true. I wished Marigold would stop talking about feelings and just tell me what to do.

'You remember last time, we were talking about guilt,' she said. Then she reminded me, in case I'd forgotten. 'I was saying that everyone in the family can think it was their fault when someone commits suicide?'

It sounded like a question, so I nodded.

'Well, guilt can be a very big block to recovery after a loved one has died. Even if we don't think it was our fault, we can still feel guilty just for being alive, when they aren't, because it doesn't seem fair.'

Every time she stopped talking, my stomach knotted up. I couldn't answer her; I couldn't even look at her, and beside everything else, I knew I was being was rude.

Maybe she would suddenly take offence – not that she showed much sign of that, sitting there so calm and patient. There was nothing sharp or dangerous about Marigold; she was soft and safe, from her pale blonde hair to her grey and silver shoes.

The minutes ticked away towards the end of the hour.

Marigold said, 'Let's talk about your writing. I guess you feel you've told Seb everything by now?'

I nodded. I hadn't actually, but the answer was nearer to yes than no.

'Did you find it helpful?'

I nodded again.

'I imagine you might be feeling a sense of loss, now that it's over.'

It wasn't a question. I waited. Marigold picked up the gel pens I'd brought back, and pushed the two new ones towards me. She took some paper from her folder.

'Keep writing to Seb,' she said. 'Just see what comes.'

It was easy writing to you last night because I wanted to tell you about what happened with Marigold. What shall I talk about now? It's five o'clock in the morning, still pitch dark outside, and I'm sitting here in my dressing gown feeling really ill.

I read in this book about bereavement that Marigold lent me that your body expresses your emotions. If a woman loses a child, she can get breast cancer because that's where it hurts – in the mothering part of her. If a man loses his wife, maybe he'll have a heart attack because his heart is breaking.

Women and girls often stop having periods when someone close to them dies – I felt a bit better when I read that, considering that's what seems to be happening to me. The book said your body can feel and express emotions you don't even know you've got.

That book got me thinking. My body has been feeling really bad lately, and I'm never usually ill. It's like I've got this hollowness inside. My stomach feels empty all the time, even when I've just eaten. Food seems to either disappear in the hollowness or refuse to go down at all, and come straight back up.

Also, I can't seem to sleep. When I lie down, my muscles won't relax and my mind can't switch off. It's like scenes from a film that keep playing over and over again, no matter how much I don't want to see them.

I mean, why did they have to do a post mortem?

They said it was 'just routine in cases like this' – an apparent suicide who didn't leave a note. I got paranoid wondering what they were looking for. Did they think someone else had done it? Stuffed the tablets into your mouth and forced you to drink the gin?

If they did, I must be the person in the frame. It was me who found you and what's more, I didn't tell anyone. Mum and Dad were so agitated about that – they kept asking me 'How long were you there? Why didn't you fetch us straight away? How could you be absolutely sure…?'

'Look at us when we're speaking to you!' they would say. 'Stop this nonsense! Say something!'

I guess they thought, being only sixteen, I couldn't tell the difference between you alive and you dead. I could have felt insulted by that, but I let it wash over me, like everything else. Not having a voice meant I didn't have to think about how I felt at all.

In the week between your death and your funeral, Nan came round every day with soup. It was steaming hot weather and the last thing any of us wanted to do was eat soup, but we did it anyway. We did lots of things we didn't want to do, such as phoning people to tell them what had happened, and making the funeral arrangements.

The house felt weird and businesslike, with Mum, Dad and Nan writing lists and ordering flowers one minute, then bursting into tears in the middle of making a cup of tea the next.

Marky slept out in the annexe, which was just as well, or else Nan might have moved in. She kept trying to talk to me and if Marky hadn't gone out there, I would have gone myself, just to get out of the house.

But Marky wanted Darius to come over every day and there was no way he would have come if he was going to be cooped up in the crazy house with the rest of us.

I spent most of that week on the computer playing games and checking your Facebook page to see what people were posting on your wall. There were things like 'RIP' and 'see you in heaven' and 'heart you always'. Stupid, stupid messages from stupid, stupid people who had probably never even met you.

If Lexi was online she usually tried to chat. She kept asking me questions, such as could she come round? She wasn't embarrassed like most people. But when I didn't answer, her messages became less frequent.

Tris sent me a postcard saying the sun was very hot and the villa had a great swimming pool. I sent him a text telling him never to get in touch with me again. On a scale of one to important, he had dropped right off the bottom. On a scale of one to lovely, I knew now that he'd never really been anywhere else.

I was dreading going to see your body again, in the funeral parlour, but Mum insisted it would help. Seeing you there would make your death feel more real, she said. The thing that put me off most was thinking about the pathologist rummaging around inside you like a burglar, digging out all your secrets. I didn't want to see your body knowing that.

Mum had already been with Dad and Nan before she took me and Marky and she told us not to worry; you looked very peaceful. We followed her up the wide front steps of the funeral parlour and into the entrance hall, which was empty except for a dark wooden reception desk and an enormous clock.

I wondered why they had that clock. I mean, it took up most of the wall in front of you as you walked in the door. It hit you in the face. Maybe it was supposed to make you focus on the way that life keeps ticking away. Everyone dies, it seemed to say; your time is coming too.

A woman in a black dress showed us through into a viewing room, and there you were. The thing I thought of when I saw you was those programmes they do when they make over someone's house while they're away. Mum was right when she said you looked peaceful, but you didn't look like you. For a start, you were wearing make-up – it was subtle, but I could definitely tell. Plus your hair was wrong – they'd given you a parting.

I didn't want to stay and neither did Marky, but Mum didn't seem to notice. 'Should we put a chess piece in the coffin beside him?' she said. 'He always looked nice in that shirt.' She got through loads of tissues.

I took Marky outside because he was getting upset,

and gave him a mint from the packet I had in my pocket. There didn't seem to be anything else to do. We waited. Mum came out. We went home.

Then finally it was the funeral. You see lots of funerals on films and TV and that's probably why, when it came to it, I felt like an actor, walking across the ugly crematorium gardens towards the concrete chapel. We had to wait in a side room until everyone else had gone in and I was worried they might not have left any room for us.

It was odd because most of the people streaming in would never have come to see you when you were alive. People like the Hastings cousins, because Dad and Uncle James were hardly ever on speaking terms you used to call it 'the Battle of Hastings' whenever they met.

There was Ms Blake from school and Mr and Mrs Blumfield from next door. Half the chess club, clustering round droopy Della as if she might collapse in a heap on the ground if they gave her enough room. Mr Arnold and most of the sixth form, crying and hugging each other.

Although the chapel was crammed, I needn't have worried because they'd left the front row empty for us. Mum and Dad, Nan, Marky and me. We all had to file past everyone else to get to our seats, while they looked round and stared at us.

We were so close to your coffin that I could almost have reached out and touched it. I knew what you looked like inside it, lying there with your face make-up and parting, but this time there was no escape and even though Marky was getting upset, we couldn't go outside.

I tried to concentrate on what the vicar was saying because it took my mind off thinking about your body, lying in that box. He kept calling you 'our brother in Jesus' which I think you would have found insulting, considering he'd never even met you and you thought religion was rubbish.

When the vicar had finished speaking, Mr Arnold stood up in front of everyone and said what a promising student you'd been and how sad the whole school community was about losing you.

After that, a girl from Y13 read a poem she'd written and then Nan read your eulogy, which was basically your life story. Several times, she had to stop because her voice kind of ran out, and the paper fluttered between her fingers as if it was struggling to get away.

Some of the gaps went on for a long time, but she didn't once look up or meet anyone's eye. She just stared down and held on to that paper really hard until she got everything under control enough to go on reading.

I had wondered, when she first stood up, why Nan was doing it and not Mum or Dad, but by the time she got to the end, I knew that neither of them would have got through it.

Finally, we all stood up to sing some hymns that nobody knew except that big spotty girl who collapsed on the May Day half marathon. Then we sat down again and everyone went quiet, waiting.

There was a click and then this funny whirring noise. An automatic door was opening up in the wall behind you and your coffin started sliding slowly through.

Nobody had thought to tell me that was going to happen. My body started to shake. I couldn't breathe. I wanted to make it stop, to jump up out of my seat and pull you back, but I just sat there shaking while you slipped away and the door slowly whirred shut again.

The family had to file out first, past all those teary eyes. Outside, there were a dozen or so floral tributes spread out along the edge of the path. We filed past them, reading all the cards. 'Dearest Duck...' Duck? Who called you that? 'To the best bridge player in the borough...' What? 'A wonderful auntie...'

We stared at them stupidly until someone realised we'd got the wrong ones, and then we all traipsed further up the path to look at yours. Mum, Dad, Nan, me and Marky left everyone else admiring the flowers and went home, so we'd be there to greet everyone when they arrived at our house.

I wished we'd done what Nan had suggested and booked a hall, because when everyone pitched up at the house it felt like an invasion. You couldn't move for people balancing paper plates full of sausage rolls and sandwiches, sipping tea and speaking in hushed voices.

They all kept saying how wonderful you were in between discussing stuff like jobs that needed doing in the garden at this time of year and where they were going on holiday. They grabbed my hands and said how sorry they were for my loss. Even if I'd been talking, I wouldn't have known what to say.

I went to my room and stayed there until everyone had gone. When I came downstairs, Dad was sitting on the patio drinking whisky. Mum and Nan were inside, clearing up, and Marky was in the annexe on his Xbox. There were no arrangements to make any more; there was nothing else to be done.

I wandered down to the potting shed. Through the green windowpanes I could see Tilly's nasturtiums, brown and shrivelled in the jar, but I couldn't bring myself to go in.

As I walked back up to the house, Dad drained his glass and said, 'I don't know if I ever really felt that close to him.'

The patio pots hadn't been watered and the leaves were dying on the stems. Most of the flowers were finished.

'If I'd loved him more, maybe he wouldn't have done it,' Dad continued.

He was drunk, but that wasn't surprising. He always got drunk after family gatherings, even under normal circumstances, didn't he?

Inside, Mum and Nan were sitting at the kitchen table. They stopped talking when I went in. Mum looked away, waiting for me to leave.

I thought, She hates me now, because I'm alive and Seb is dead.

'Suicide is a permanent solution to a temporary problem.' I read that on a website. Also, 'Most people who once thought about killing themselves are now glad to be alive.' So, you'd have been glad, then, if I'd told Mum about your secret stash and she'd marched you off to see a psychiatrist or something, or at least made Nan keep a better eye on her pills.

Looking on websites didn't make me feel better but once I'd started, I couldn't seem to stop. I found out lots of random things about suicide. For example, you were lucky to survive that first attempt. Apparently, even if you get your stomach pumped and seem to be recovering, you can still die of paracetamol poisoning a few days later because your liver packs up, and it's a horrible way to go.

I found out there are three stages of suicide – struggle, planning and resolve. In the first stage, the person is agonising about whether to do it or not, and they might seem quite agitated. If your body expresses your emotions like the bereavement book said, then I guess that might have been the real reason you got your lumps.

If the planning stage came after that, you must have been working out the details of your death at about the same time that me and Lexi were organising your party.

Once a person has finished the planning, they often seem unusually calm and happy. They might start giving their treasured possessions away. You came and sat on my bed; you talked to me about Tris; you made your lists.

There was so much information but none of it explained why. Some experts said teenagers didn't understand that death was permanent, but that wasn't you. You weren't an idiot.

Some experts said teenagers were obsessed with celebrity and would do anything to grab the headlines, even killing themselves. But that wasn't you either. Everyone expected you would do great things and get really famous anyway.

Some experts said it was boredom or lack of money that made young people decide their lives were too rubbish to bother going on with. But you had Chess Central and Della, A-levels and Cambridge, and okay, we didn't live on Millionaires' Row but it was hardly Scum City either.

I found out there were suicide chat rooms, with mission statements that sounded calm and sensible, like you. They said things such as 'we don't judge' and 'suicide is a personal choice' and 'there is nothing immoral or irrational about taking your own life'.

In these chat rooms everyone talked about suicide as if it was an ordinary everyday thing, like going to the shops. They actually called it 'catching the bus'. Trawling the messages, I wondered whether you were in there behind one of the names – ghost, nearligone, TJ, darkstar. But they didn't sound like the kind of people you would want to hang out with at all.

Nan was round our house a lot in the weeks after the funeral because Mum had stopped shopping and cooking, and someone had to look after us. She kept trying to get me to talk. She said it would make me feel better.

Really? I thought. Is talking going to bring Seb back? Is it going to make Marky remember how to smile? Is it going to make Mum stop acting weird? Is it going to mean Dad stops getting drunk all the time?

Because he never sobered up after the funeral, Seb. He just kept drinking. I expect he was drunk the day he went back to work. That was probably the real reason he got sent home, though his boss was too kind to say so. She told him she thought he was still understandably really upset, and had probably come back to work too soon.

'Take however much time you need,' she told him. Dad said he didn't need time, he needed work, but she didn't give him the choice, and that did nothing to improve his mood.

He hung around the house all day every day like a bear with a sore head, or rather a bear with a massive hangover, and he kept having a go at Marky and me, every chance he got.

If Marky lost his bus money, or didn't eat all his supper, or complained about not having the right sports kit, Dad was all over it.

'Bloody kids, you give them everything, you put your own life on hold, and what do they do? They throw it back in your face!'

I didn't even have to do anything to set him off. Just the fact that I wasn't talking made him mad at me.

'Where are you going? Say something! Look at me when I'm talking to you! Bloody kids. No bloody manners.'

Mum tried to stop him laying into us at first, but then she gave up and told us we'd just have to try and take no notice. She said it was just the drink talking and he didn't really mean it.

Well all I can say is, he did. He looked at us now the way Mum used to look at Lexi, like Lexi was something she had trodden in. It was you he was angry with, but you weren't there, so he took it out on Marky and me.

He knew he was doing it too, because one night I walked in on him in his study when he was drunk, and I could see he'd been crying, so I thought, I'd better get out of here, but before I could go anywhere he grabbed my arm and muttered something that sounded like sorry. Which was all very well but when he'd sobered up, nothing had changed.

He took it out on Mum sometimes as well, telling her you wouldn't have been such a weak waste of space if she hadn't mollycoddled you. It was nothing he hadn't said before, but he said it in such a bitter way, and Mum didn't argue. She didn't respond at all.

From time to time she did have a go at him for drinking. She hid his car keys to stop him killing anybody by driving drunk. She told him: 'You shouldn't drink. It makes you nasty,' which was true. You wouldn't believe how different he was, Seb. You wouldn't have recognised him.

Families are supposed to pull together in a crisis, but ours fell apart and kept on falling. Nan tried to mend things by making nice meals and getting us to sit down in the evening and eat as a family, but all that meant was that every day ended really badly, and it was all my fault.

It would have been all right if they'd left me alone, but eating was a struggle and talking was impossible, and everyone was on my case. Mum was mostly worried about me offending Nan, saying things like 'Nan's gone to a lot of trouble to make this lovely dinner for us' and 'I hope you're going to eat that broccoli, it's full of vitamins' and 'a thank you wouldn't go amiss'.

Nan wasn't bothered about being offended, but she was worried about me. 'You have to eat something to keep your strength up' she would say, and 'you're looking very pale today' and 'would you like me to make you some pasta instead?'

Dad wasn't worried about anyone. He'd sit there fuming until it all got too much for him, and then he'd blow. 'What's wrong with you, Jessica?' He spat out my name. 'It's just plain rude, not answering when you're spoken to!'

The best I could do was look down at the tablecloth and go on eating, slowly and steadily, trying not to choke. Eventually, Dad would give up and turn his fire on everyone else.

'Why are you letting her get away with this? Her behaviour is appalling! In my day...' Blah, blah, blah.

I wished we could all eat separately, like they do at Lexi's. At least, it seemed to me, a family that eats separately wouldn't notice so much when one of them was missing.

And you were totally and utterly missing at our family mealtimes, Seb. Nobody talked about you, because that would mean acknowledging you weren't around. There were no present tenses now for you, no 'Seb's got a summer job/ doing well in the summer chess challenge/ staying over at Della's...'

There were no future tenses, no 'Seb's going to give you a lift tonight/ play for his college/ see Della at weekends when he goes up to Cambridge…' There were only past tenses for you now, and that was how it would be for ever.

So nobody talked about you, and that meant you were nowhere. You weren't here, and you weren't gone. You were in limbo, like a ghost, and we were all afraid to look at you.

If home was bad after your funeral, school was even worse. There were only a few weeks left before the summer holidays so it felt kind of pointless, and everyone was trying to be nice to me, when all I wanted was to be left alone.

Mrs Hardiman hijacked me the minute I walked in the door on my first day back and asked me to come to her office. How often does a Head Teacher do that? She said the whole school community had been devastated by your tragic death.

All the teachers were aware of my sad loss, she said, and our class had had an opportunity to talk about it in a special meeting, because lots of people were upset and suicide was such a complicated and sensitive subject.

She told me not to worry about missing my last few GCSE exams. They would give me a pass because of special circumstances and it wouldn't stop me doing my chosen A-Levels and applying for university.

'I think it might be really helpful for you to have a chat with our school counsellor,' she said. 'Would you like me to fix that up?'

It was the first time she'd asked me a question and until that point I don't think she noticed that I hadn't said anything. When I didn't answer, she said I didn't have to decide right away, and I could come back and see her any time I wanted to. Her door was always open.

Outside in the corridor several teachers took me to one side to tell me they had heard my 'bad news' and were really sorry. Mr Sharma actually did look on the edge of tears.

When I got to the common room, everyone stopped talking and there was like this whispery hush before they started coming to talk to me. It felt bad watching them struggle to find the right words, knowing I had absolutely nothing to say back.

Over the next few days, some people tried to talk to me about Seb again, and others tried talking about other things, just to be friendly, but in the end I guess they didn't know what to do with me, and had to give up. Even Lexi eventually gave up and left me alone at school, which came as a massive relief.

Sometimes she talked to me online after we got home, and the fact that I only ever managed the occasional yes, no or sorry didn't seem to put her off at all. I suppose yes, no and sorry was enough to tell her I was there, and I was listening.

If Joely thought she was going to be Lexi's new best friend in class now there was a vacancy, that wasn't happening, because of the new girl, Alyssa. She was a year older than us, because she'd flunked out of her old school and had to resit her GCSE's, and she turned up at for the last few weeks of term to get settled in before starting A-Levels.

She was as skinny as a catwalk model and everything she said was, like, in questions?

Alyssa told us, 'Like, my Mum and Dad split up?' She said, 'We've got this, like, house in the Village? My brother's at university? He's, like, got a car?'

They must've been mega rich before her parents split up if they could still afford to live in the Village. But money isn't everything, as they say and, judging by Alyssa, too much of it can make a person believe the whole world should revolve around them.

When I first met her I thought Alyssa was, like, such a drama queen? But it was one of Lexi's golden rules that you had to be nice to new people, at least until you knew them well enough to decide if they were worth it. So she took Alyssa under her wing, and before you could say 'traitor' they seemed to have become best mates.

I couldn't really blame Lexi, though. I wasn't hanging around with her at break times and she got really pissed off with me when she forgot I wasn't speaking and tried to talk to me at school.

When you aren't talking, it's as if you aren't joined up to anyone. You notice that conversation is like invisible threads that attach people to each other, and pull them along. When you aren't talking, you kind of drift. It actually feels quite peaceful. Things can be happening all around, but nothing seems to affect you.

When you aren't talking, you start to see things differently. Some days, I sat in the empty corridor outside the library all through dinner time, just looking at the letters on the library door. Each letter with its own mysterious geometry. The gaps between.

Random things that I had never really noticed before held my attention now, and I felt soothed by them. I had a sense of belonging, as I sank into the background with them.

I often thought about Schrödinger's cat. If you were to put a cat in a box and send it out into space, so nobody could see it or smell it or hear it or touch it, then would that cat still exist?

I'd said I thought Schrödinger should get a life – of course the cat still existed! Now you were just like Schrödinger's cat. No one could see you, or touch you or hear you, but that didn't mean you no longer existed.

In the early days it had been enough just knowing you were somewhere, but as the days went by, I wanted more. I wanted to see you. I had questions to ask you, such as where were you now and what was it like? I wanted to ask you – why did you do it? Why didn't you leave us a note?

Mum thought it was because of the cancer. She said that had made death part of your thinking even when you were little, in a way that it wasn't part of ours. Or sometimes she said maybe it was because they'd pushed you too hard – or maybe they hadn't pushed you hard enough and you'd felt they didn't care.

Dad banged on about 'young people today' being stupid and not knowing how lucky they were, so presumably he blamed it on society in general.

I wanted to ask you, 'When did you know you were going to do it? Did you already know on the day I found your stash of sleeping pills? Did you lie to me?' I wanted you to tell me no. It felt important.

In the bereavement book it said a lot of people actually see the dead person and talk to them after they've died, which means that they must have seen a ghost. I wasn't so sceptical about ghosts any more, because sometimes I seemed to physically feel you close by, as if I had a sixth sense.

It wasn't scary like in the film. I didn't think you were going to suddenly appear in a doorway all covered in gore and grab me. Why should you be any different now from how you had always been? The feeling was so strong at times that when I turned to look I could hardly believe you weren't there.

I trawled the net for information about ghosts. People talked about feeling the air go cold, as if the coldness of the dead person's body could infect it. They talked about hearing footsteps in an empty house.

Well, sometimes I was sure I heard your footsteps on the stairs and your voice saying my name, but I knew it couldn't really be you, so I guessed the sound must be printed on the air, like a footprint in the snow, still there after the foot has gone.

Shadows and echoes. I wanted to see you again. I wanted to talk to you. I wanted it so much it physically hurt. I decided to go out to the potting shed at night when everyone else was asleep, just like I'd done on the night you died.

No one had been in there since they had taken you away. That was where you had last been, where the print of you would be freshest.

Once I'd made up my mind, I had to wait for the full moon, because I'd read that was the time when you were most likely to see a ghost. I would go at midnight, if everyone was in bed by then.

I would take the picnic blankets, just like I did before, and wear the same pyjamas. Of course, it would be dark this time, and really spooky. But I would sit on the cushions and wait for you; I would wait as long as it took. And you would come.

The day of the full moon, I was already feeling edgy and, to make matters worse, Alyssa really pissed me off. She heard me throwing up in the toilets and, in her role as resident expert on everything, on account of being a year older than the rest of us, she told everyone I had bulimia.

Then that creep Joely told Ms Jury and she took me to one side and gave me a talk about why bulimia is a bad idea.

'It might feel like a way of taking control of your life right now, Jess,' she said. She had obviously been reading her psychology books. 'It might seem like a solution, but soon it'll just become another problem.'

I was spitting feathers. Okay, I threw up; okay I sometimes felt sick at the moment, but I did not have bulimia. When I got home, I went straight online.

Lexi said: *Don't be cross about Ms Jury knowing you've got bulimia. We think you might need some help.*

She said Alyssa only told everyone about me throwing up because she was worried about me. Bulimia was a very dangerous thing, as I might not be aware, and anyway it was Joely who actually took it upon herself to tell.

It was starting. Lexi was taking Alyssa's side against me. She said I should listen to Alyssa because she was older than us, plus she was really clever. Lexi was always impressed by clever people.

She only flunked her GCSE's the first time because

*of her parents splitting up, but she's predicted all A*s now. I went to pieces when my parents split up too, so I know how that feels.*

It seemed like the two of them had a lot in common. It was making me want to be sick again. Lexi must have been psychic or something because she stopped banging on about Saint Alyssa and sent me a video clip of Digger.

He was the runt of Doris's litter, and to be honest he looked more like a fat little rat than a puppy. Everyone had been amazed when they'd managed to find a home for him, but now his new owners had gone off the idea and brought him back.

Doris was doing her best to ignore him and he didn't seem to be taking the hint, so there was a fair bit of pushing and growling going on.

Do you think that Marky might want him? Lexi asked.

I thought, Why not? Now you and your lumps were out of the picture, there was nothing to stop us getting another dog. I put my laptop, which was once your laptop, on the bed and got up to change out of my uniform.

Time slowed down. I could feel my mind trying to process what I was seeing through the window. The potting shed had gone.

Dad was having a bonfire on the brown earth down by the butterfly patch. He was leaning on the rake, watching the flames. I went downstairs. The back door was open and the kitchen smelt of smoke. I started to walk slowly across the lawn.

There was a pale rectangle on the end wall, where the potting shed had been. The concrete foundation was cracked and pitted. I guessed Dad had tried to break it up with the sledgehammer, which was propped up against the wall with the broom. All tidy. Done and dusted.

Dad looked over his shoulder at me.

'It's time to move on,' he said. 'That old potting shed was a constant reminder.'

Behind him, the bonfire flared, which made him turn back to check it was all right. He poked at it with the rake, and some sparks sprayed up. They burnt out, turning black on the air, before floating down all around us. One of them was big enough for me to see it was a fragment of fabric from the old cushions.

Dad said. 'I'm going to stop drinking and sort myself out. I need to get back to work.'

I stepped closer to the fire. My Christmas cracker picture frame was near the edge, with flames licking around it. They had eaten away the picture of Tilly, and now there was nothing left in the middle but a black hole. Nearer to the centre of the fire, I thought I saw a beer tin, so Dad hadn't stopped drinking yet.

'It's time you sorted yourself out too,' Dad said.

I would never see you again now. The print of you was burning up just as your body had been burnt, behind the sliding doors in the crematorium.

'Say something, Jess. For Jesus' sake.'

I felt like that woman who got stabbed in the High Street last year – we read about it in the paper. She thought someone had just shoved past her, and went on walking home without even realising he'd actually stuck a knife in her back.

When she took off her coat and saw the blood, it hit her that she was hurt. Imagine. Blood pouring out of you all that time, and you don't even know. How crazy is that?

All the niggly nasty things Dad had said to me since the day of your funeral came back in a rush. I remembered every word as if he had just said it, but this time, I felt the knife go in. And Tris in the car, and you in the potting shed – I saw the blood and knew that I was hurt.

A piece of wood dropped out of the fire. Dad pushed it back with his foot.

'Mum thinks we could plant a tree here for Seb,' he said. 'What do you think?'

I thought, He wants to go back to normal, as if nothing has happened between us.

I turned to go.

'Say something.'

I went on walking.

'It's going to be better now,' he called after me. 'A fresh start. I promise.'

It was sausage and mash for supper. There's something about mashed potato that makes it hard to swallow, and I had a lot of trouble getting it down. I noticed Mum kept looking at me and then looking at Dad. Even Marky was giving me funny looks. Probably, Ms Jury had been on the phone.

But it wasn't my stomach this time that felt empty and sick; it was all of me. I put down my knife and fork. I wanted to go, but I couldn't get up. Mum gestured to the others and they took their food into the living room. We heard them turn on the TV.

Mum said, 'Are you upset about Dad taking the potting shed down?'

I looked at her. She told me she hadn't really wanted him to do it either, but maybe it was for the best, on account of he did seem happier now, as if he had turned a corner, which he needed to do. Which we all needed to do, blah blah blah.

She said he wasn't a well man; his blood pressure was through the roof since he'd been off work and anything that made him feel better had to be a good thing. I went on looking at her.

Mum said it might be hard for me to understand, because I was a bit of a sentimentalist, like Nan, and maybe I would have wanted to keep the potting shed for ever, like she'd kept the old camper van after Grampy died, even though everyone knew she would never go on any trips in it again now she was on her own. It was still on the drive at the side of her house where it had always been, but the tyres were flat and the inside was full of flowers, like a greenhouse.

'Some people like to keep things and some people don't,' Mum said. 'We've all got a different point of view.'

I thought, So how come you just got rid of the potting shed and I didn't get any say in it?

But straight away I realised that was just stupid, because how can you have your say when you aren't saying anything at all?

I woke up in the night because my foot had gone to sleep. It was hanging over the side of the bed. I moved my leg to haul it back in, but it was so numb I couldn't tell whether I'd managed to get it back under the quilt or not. I sat up to rub it. Nothing. I hit it with my fist. The feeling started to come back in a shower of pins and needles.

The moonlight was streaming in through the window. It was just after midnight and everyone was asleep. I should have been down in the potting shed by now, waiting for you to come. Except we didn't have a potting shed any more, did we? My whole body seemed to come alive with prickles of pain. I didn't like it. I wanted it to stop.

I turned the light on and lay staring up at the ceiling. Whiteness is very soothing, like the soft weight of the quilt over the length of your body. If you look at whiteness for long enough, all your senses shut down. Sounds become faint and far away. Your mind goes blank.

I must have dozed off because the sound of Mum trying to get Marky out of bed woke me up. I knew she'd come and get me up next, so I fixed my gaze on the ceiling and waited. She tapped on the door, came into the room, pulled the curtains back.

'Time to get up, Jess.'

She knew, because I went on staring at the ceiling, that I wouldn't be going to school that day; I knew she wouldn't have time to argue about it because she had to get to work. She was cross with me, but she went.

I heard Dad moving about in the kitchen and waited till he'd gone out before I went downstairs. He'd left a note on the table – *Back about 3.*

Whatever.

Television can do that whiteness thing as well, so I sat in front of it all day long and let it make me numb. Even when Marky came in almost wetting himself with excitement because Lexi had seen him on the bus and asked if he wanted to take Digger, and Mum had miraculously said he could, I managed to stay wholly focused on *The Simpsons*.

When they brought Digger home in a shoebox two hours later, I didn't allow myself to be distracted from *Building Bathrooms*, and by the time I went to bed, I was feeling as blank as the ceiling.

The next day was Saturday and I didn't get up.

Mum brought me a cup of tea, which sat on my bedside table growing a skin until Nan arrived and I couldn't stay in bed any more, because we all had to be there for the planting of your tree.

Dad had dug the earth over where the bonfire had been and made a hole. He had a can in his hand, as usual, but I noticed it wasn't beer; he was drinking lemonade. Like that would last.

The tree was spindly and no taller than Marky, and it looked way too small for the gigantic hole. Dad said he had chosen a mountain ash because it would have white flowers in the spring and red berries in the summer, and also, he liked the idea of mountains growing from ashes – or some shit like that. We stood round and watched while he pulled the tree out of its pot and placed it in the hole.

When Dad started heaping the soil in over the roots, Digger went nuts; Marky could hardly hold onto him because he was so keen to join in.

Mum said, 'He's just like Tilly was when she was a puppy.' But he wasn't Tilly, was he?

Dad stepped back and we stood in a line, looking at the tree. Nan was saying we could tie ribbons to the branches if we wanted to, which would be like prayers for you. I couldn't see what there was to pray for. Praying wouldn't bring you back.

Digger wriggled like a hyperactive eel in Marky's arms, but otherwise nobody moved. Mum and Dad were separate, not touching, not trying to comfort each other. I remembered they hadn't always been like that.

Things were moving on, just like Dad wanted. We had this tree now, where we used to have the potting shed. We had Digger where we used to have Tilly. We used to have a life where things seemed to work more or less okay, and now we had a life where everything hurt.

The pins and needles started up behind my eyes and I pressed my hands into them to make it stop. Mum tried to make me go inside and have a cup of hot chocolate, but I was rooted like the little mountain ash; I wasn't going anywhere.

Nan stayed outside with me. 'Your mum's really worried about you,' she said. 'We all are.'

I didn't want her to talk to me. She came towards me but I stopped her with a look.

'Why don't we talk to each other any more, Jess? We always used to.'

I waited for the silence to settle.

Nan said, 'Sometimes bad things happen, and we can't prevent it. All we can do is try to cope and, when it's over, learn to let go. Holding on to pain just hurts all the people who care about us. There are lots of people who care about you, Jess. Your mum and dad, Marky, Lexi, all your other friends... Me.'

I wanted to talk to Nan. I wouldn't tell her how bad I was feeling, as in I wished I could go to sleep and never have to wake up again, because that would just freak her out.

I would say, 'I haven't had the painters in for three months now.' That's what she called periods, 'having the painters in'.

I would say, 'I feel sick all the time and I'm scared.' But the words didn't come.

Nan went up to the house to make us a drink and I stood on the square of concrete where the potting shed had been. I thought of you hiding Grampy's cigar box out there, and creeping out later in the dark.

I imagined you opening the box, and seeing the white sleeping tablets lit up by the moon or perhaps, if it was cloudy, by the lights streaming out from the back of the house.

Because we were all there, maybe reading or chatting online, or watching TV, or asleep in our beds – and you were out here feeling like nobody loved you enough to care whether you lived or died. That's how it must have been because otherwise, how could you have done it?

Nan had said I needed to find a way of getting through this for the sake of all the people who loved me, but when she had rattled off the list, do you know what, Seb? I didn't feel as if any of them loved me at all.

FOUR

'How have you been this week?' Marigold asked.

It wasn't a yes-or-no question, and it felt like she was trying to trick me into speaking. Maybe she thought that starting straight in with it when I'd hardly had a chance to even sit down would give her the element of surprise.

I took her blue and brown gel pens out of my bag, placed them on the low table beside us and pushed them towards her.

'Are you still writing to Seb?'

I nodded.

'Do you still feel that it's helping?'

I frowned. I hadn't really asked myself that question. Writing to you had become just something I did, to pass the endless silent hours, like an addiction or something.

Marigold waited, but after a few moments, when I still hadn't nodded or shaken my head, she picked up last week's gel pens and dropped them into her bag.

'Last time, we were talking about sadness,' Marigold said.

I was still trying to work out whether writing to

155

you was helping or not, and I realised I was probably feeling worse now than when I started. It was getting much harder to keep things calm and numb; I had to really focus. Was that because of seeing Marigold, or because of writing to you?

I certainly hadn't wanted to come to this session, because I was feeling 'out of sorts' as Nan would say. My face felt hot, and my legs were so restless it was all I could do to keep them still.

I looked at the stain on the carpet, but that wouldn't stay still either. The dust on the skirting board, a new scuff on the wall, a screwed-up piece of paper someone had dropped on the floor.

The dead fly on the windowsill, which would have held my attention before, couldn't hold my gaze now.

Marigold wasn't wearing the grey shoes with the silver trim, but plain black ankle boots with low pointy heels. All her colours were different today, not soft blues and pinks, but black trousers and a fitted white shirt, which I didn't like at all.

What was the message in her clothes? Was she going to tell me she didn't want to see me any more?

Marigold said, 'We talked about guilt as well as sadness, particularly what we call "survivor guilt", which can make us feel bad about still being alive after somebody close to us has died.'

I caught a movement on the windowsill out of the corner of my eye. The fly wasn't dead. It was just stuck upside down, and had probably worn itself out trying to get the right way up again. It gave a short, weak buzz and thrashed its legs around, then stopped.

'Today, I want to talk about something else that can make people feel guilty when they lose someone, and that is anger. It doesn't seem right to feel angry when somebody dies, does it? But everyone does.'

Not me, I thought. This time, she was way off the mark.

'Some people feel angry with God, and maybe that feels sinful,' Marigold said. 'Do you believe in God, Jess?'

I shook my head.

Marigold said, 'At some point, nearly everyone feels angry with the person who has died.'

Nearly everyone, but not me. How could I feel angry with you? You had cancer and a false foot, and lumps; you had a girlfriend who kept splitting up with you.

If I was going to feel angry with anyone it would be Mum for killing Tilly, and Dad for turning into a nasty old drunk and burning down the potting shed so I could never see you again. It would be Nan for giving me bad advice. It would be Tris for... for... Marigold didn't know about any of the other stuff and I suddenly wished I could tell her.

'It's natural to feel angry,' Marigold said. 'We get angry with the people close to us when they're alive, so why should it be any different when they die?'

I did not feel angry with you. Why did she keep saying this? Stain, dust, scuff, paper... stain, dust, scuff, paper...

'Feeling angry with someone who has died is part of the grieving process, yet we can sometimes feel so bad about it that we idealise the person, and make him impossible to be angry with.'

Stain, dust, scuff, paper... Stop it, Marigold. Stop!

'We might even forget about the anger we felt before he died as well.'

I hadn't forgotten anything. She was laying all this stuff on me, knowing that I couldn't set her straight, because I wasn't talking.

'It's all right to feel angry,' Marigold said.

There was a sudden furious burst of buzzing from the fly, which went skittering across the windowsill on its back and tumbled down onto the floor.

'The thing about anger is we need it. It gives us the energy to survive. I sense you have a lot of anger inside you right now, Jess.'

It wasn't a question, and I didn't respond. The fly moved unsteadily a few inches across the carpet, towards the screwed-up piece of paper.

Marigold said I should 'get in touch with my anger', as if I could simply send it a text. She said that would make me feel better. But then, she didn't know about Dad. He was in touch with his anger all right. His blood pressure had gone through the roof, he was so angry all the time.

After three days on lemonade instead of beer, he'd gone back to work again and completely lost his rag with someone in his office, hitting the table, throwing stuff around. She'd made a formal complaint, which was fair enough, and he'd been suspended until the results of an enquiry. He might even lose his job.

'You can't sack someone for having a short fuse,' he said. 'They needn't think they can get rid of me like that!' Then he drank a whole bottle of whisky in one evening. So much for sorting himself out. So much for making a fresh start.

Marigold took a clean stack of paper out of her bag, and two new gel pens, this time red and black. She put them on the table and pushed them towards me. The absolute best way to handle anger was simply to express it, she said.

'Expressing your anger isn't about being destructive or aggressive – it's about speaking up for yourself. If you don't do that, no one else will know how you feel, and sometimes you might not even know how you feel yourself.'

She was doing my head in. Where was the fly? It seemed to have crawled under the screwed-up paper. Was it just resting, or dead?

We were hardly ten minutes into the session and she wasn't leaving enough silences; the hands on the clock seemed to be jerking round in fits and starts, not slicing time up into slow, equal pieces.

'We have to express and feel our anger before we can let it go,' Marigold said.

Backwards and forwards the second hand went, this way and that. My foot started tapping on the floor, all on its own. I didn't stop it.

'When we really feel and express our anger, then we can let it go.'

I was NOT ANGRY with you! Why couldn't she get that through her thick head?

I grabbed the paper and the two new gels, and walked out.

I can't believe I walked out on Marigold like that, Seb, but come to think of it, I knew I wasn't in the mood to see her today. Like I said, I was feeling out of sorts before I even went in.

I'm not really in the mood for writing to you either, but still. Where was I up to? Oh, yes... Dad burning the potting shed down and putting that poxy little tree in its place.

I couldn't face going back to school for the last few days of term, so I didn't. There was nothing on the calendar for the holidays except your A-level results on 13th August and my GCSE results on the 20th, which were marked with gold star stickers, and two weeks of 'Portugal', crossed out.

It was the wettest August on record, so we were indoors most of the time, me in my bedroom and Marky in the annexe with Darius and Digger. Dad was either drunk or obsessing about his official enquiry, which meant Nan had to come round every day to keep an eye on us.

Nan had stopped trying to get me to talk to her when she saw me, but just chatted normally, as if I was joining in. Not that it was much of an issue because I mostly stayed up in my room on my own.

I did some painting, read some books, watched some films, played some games, and time moved at about the same speed as a glacier, one hundredth of a millimetre per seven billion years (you'd probably know the right numbers and not have to make them up).

Sometimes, Lexi still came online, but she never suggested meeting. It would have been awkward with the not-talking thing and anyway, her mum had got her a holiday job four days a week in the leisure centre. In the evenings she hung out with Monk.

Lexi said Monk had started working full time in the job he'd been doing every Saturday since he was sixteen.

He wishes he'd left school and gone full time sooner. He says A-levels are for losers.

Lexi had decided she wasn't going to university either, because there wasn't any point. I thought maybe the point of going to university might be precisely because if you didn't, you could end up stuck in the same kind of job you'd been doing since you were sixteen.

Once or twice, she talked about Tris. She said someone ought to teach 'that scumbag' a lesson for spreading it round about us having sex. She didn't even know the half of it.

Monk's got a plan, she wrote.

I didn't share Lexi's confidence in Monk. The thing about plans is that, in the wrong hands, they can backfire, and this one did. Or maybe, not so much backfire as fizzle out.

Somehow, Monk got a picture of Tris, lying in the gutter wearing nothing but his socks. I don't know whether Monk and his mates deliberately got him drunk and stripped him, and I didn't want to know. I mean Tris was, after all, a person who liked to get naked in the rain, so it was just possible they might have simply chanced upon him, doing his thing.

Anyway, Monk sent the picture to Tris, with a message saying that if he didn't apologise to me immediately and publicly admit he was a scumbag, he would make sure it went viral.

I was pretty cross with Monk, because I never asked him to stick his nose in. I didn't want an apology because I knew Tris wasn't sorry, so it wouldn't be worth shit. I was also a hundred per cent aware that he was a scumbag so I didn't need him to confirm it.

Tris must have assumed I was behind it because

he sent a message to both of us saying, *If that picture gets out so will this one.*

At first glance, it didn't look like you; I had to look really closely to see that it was. You were sprawled on some cushions in a room I didn't recognise with two people I'd never seen before, passing a joint.

How was it possible? You didn't even drink. You didn't even eat junk food, come to that. Plus I recognized your T-shirt. It was the one you bought at Easter, and after Easter you weren't supposed to be doing anything then except revision, exams and seeing Della.

Lexi was online. *Monk's just shown me that pic of Seb. I'm so sorry, Jess.*

But I knew it was a fake; it had to be. So I got rid of it, Seb.

Nan made a special celebration cake for your results day, just like she would have done if you'd still been alive. She said it would be a bittersweet day for Mum and Dad, because although they'd obviously be full of pride, they'd also feel more than ever what a waste it was that you worked so hard and now you weren't here to reap the rewards and go to Cambridge. For me, it was just another ordeal to get through, and cake was not going to help.

Dad walked to school in the morning to collect the envelope from the office, but he didn't want to open it until everyone was there. Mum cancelled her meeting so she could get home early, and Nan fussed around until we were finally all sitting down together.

Dad slit open the envelope with his knife and took out the letter. His hands were shaking as he unfolded it. He read it, then just stared at it and went on staring, until Mum gave up waiting for him to pass it over and took it off him.

'What?' said Nan. 'What's wrong?'

You know what was wrong, don't you Seb? You must have known all along, because it can't be easy to sit five A-levels and fail every single one of them. That takes some serious slacking.

'I don't understand,' said Dad.

He stood up and went out into the garden, even though it was pouring with rain. Mum followed him. Nan cut the cake, as if she was a robot and had been programmed to do it, which meant me, Marky and Darius had to eat it.

We still had half the summer holidays to get through, with only my GCSE results to look forward to but, in a weird way, your spectacular failure made whatever I achieved seem unimportant now, just as your brilliant successes always had before. (In case you're wondering, Seb, I did pass all the ones I took, and Nan put us through another ordeal by cake).

I wiped the memory of your results day like I'd wiped that photo Tris sent me, because I didn't want it in my head, it was too confusing. I was like Dad; I didn't understand.

But here's a weird thing. Now I'm writing it down,

I feel like I'm starting to understand things a whole lot better.

I understand that you let us all believe you were studying hard to get into Cambridge when, all the time, you knew it wasn't true.

I understand that you assured me you weren't going to take those tablets when you knew that was exactly what you were going to do.

You let me think you cared about what happened to me, and we were going to be close again, when the gifts you had on your list were goodbye gifts, and you knew it.

You let me think you were at Della's that night, when you sneaked round the back to the potting shed.

Lie, after lie, after lie. It was all lies. How could you do it, Seb? What did we do to deserve it?

Last night, writing all that stuff to you about Monk's stupid plan and Tris's picture of you off your face, and your results day, got me all stirred up, and I couldn't sleep for thinking about your lies.

In the small hours of the morning, I decided I wasn't going to write to you any more, whatever Marigold says, because it wasn't helping and anyway, I'd told you everything, right through from your party last Easter to the end of the summer term, the horrible school holiday and Mr Baginski making me see Marigold the minute I came back and started Sixth Form.

But I've had a really weird couple of days since then, Seb, and I've just got to tell you about it. It started with me being late for school because, having lain awake most of the night, I slept through my alarm.

Being late meant I couldn't sit in my usual place in English because Alyssa had taken it, but I didn't care. I didn't feel part of anything, so sitting at the back seemed kind of better in a way.

Ms de Rosa made her usual dramatic entrance, wearing a red jacket over a black dress that was far too young for her and rattling her bracelets. Her hair was freshly dyed – she'd gone back to black – and her eye make-up was seeping into her wrinkles.

'Good Morning!' she boomed, projecting to the back of the class as if she were performing at the National Theatre.

'*Romeo and Juliet!*' Ms de Rosa held the book up in front of us and paraded up and down. 'We have now reached the dramatic climax!'

When she spoke, you could actually hear the exclamation marks.

'Who would like to sum up for us, as simply as possible, how our 'star-crossed lovers' came to die?'

You could hear the inverted commas, too.

'Alyssa!'

She hadn't even needed to put her hand up – Ms de Rosa just assumed that she would know. The words 'teacher's' and 'pet' sprung to mind, but everyone else seemed impressed as Alyssa went rattling through the plot.

'Romeo and Juliet can't marry each other because their families don't get on, and Juliet's father says she's got to marry Paris. She takes a magic potion which will put her to sleep and make everyone think she's dead in order to get out of it.

'Romeo doesn't know what she's done, so when he finds her he thinks she's died, and he kills himself because he doesn't want to live without her. Then she wakes up, finds Romeo dying, and kills herself with his dagger. After that, the two families see the error of their ways, and stop feuding with each other.'

'What a wonderful summary!' Ms de Rosa cried. 'Succinct and to the point! It highlights beautifully the circular action of the play, from the opening feud to its final resolution.' She sat on the corner of her desk. 'Now, how does the character of Romeo lead to the outcome?'

Lexi put her hand up in her usual half-hearted way, with her elbow still on the table. She said, 'He's very hot-headed. He doesn't wait to make sure that Juliet's really dead.'

Ms de Rosa nodded vigorously. Romeo was always ready to spring into action, she gushed. It was part of his 'heroic nature'.

It seemed to me that it was part of his 'loser nature' because if life was a series of moments, like Marigold said, then what kind of loser couldn't handle just one single moment of feeling terrible?

'What else?' said Ms de Rosa.

Nobody put up their hand, so Lexi carried on. 'He's brave,' she said. 'He's not afraid to die.'

Brave? I felt the skin tighten all the way across the top of my head. What was brave about throwing in the towel the minute the going got tough? And how could Lexi have seen first-hand what all of us had gone through and still not understand?

Brave was getting up in the morning when it felt like no one cared and there was no point and nothing would ever feel right again. Brave was holding on, waiting for the endless moment to pass.

Joely put up her hand – wherever Lexi led, she was bound to follow.

'He's very romantic,' she said, in her most annoying mushy voice. 'He'd rather die than live without his love.'

Some people groaned and grinned at each other, because Joely famously fancied the actor who played Romeo in the film; when we'd watched it in class, his death scene had sent her into an actual swoon.

I looked at the wall. It was pitted and marked. Not blank; not white enough. How could anyone say that suicide was romantic? Call me stupid, but I thought romance was supposed to be related to love, which is about caring and cherishing, right? Suicide is about abandoning everyone who loves you for ever.

But Ms de Rosa liked Joely's point. She reckoned

that Romeo was the most famous lover in the language, and his suicide was what elevated him to the role of the 'great romantic hero'. I looked at the white ceiling. It was cut into squares by polystyrene tiles; too busy, too broken.

'Anyone else?' said Ms de Rosa.

Alyssa said, in a random sort of way, like someone who thinks they're so interesting they don't have to stick to the point, 'It's a beautiful scene. Two lovers, united in death.' I thought I was going to chuck.

This was so-called brilliant Alyssa, our new resident expert on life, love and everything on account of she'd been through so much – and what had she learnt? She had stuck her fingers down her throat and slit her arms with razors and she still thought there could be something beautiful about killing yourself. And they all just sat there soaking it up.

Suicide wasn't beautiful – I had seen it. It was cold and lonely. Life was beautiful, and we took it completely for granted, we hardly even noticed it – the sound of time, the air moving in and out, the sheer abundance of things that we could see and smell and touch and hear and taste. The invisible threads that connected us all together. How could it be beautiful to throw all that away?

Ms de Rosa congratulated Alyssa on an excellent observation. The beauty of the scene, she said, was underlined by the fact that the lovers' sacrifice led to the final reconciliation between their families.

169

It was stupid. Stupid, stupid, stupid! What kind of idiot could believe that Romeo and Juliet killing themselves would ever have led to any kind of happy ending? The Capulets would have blamed Romeo for Juliet's death and the Montagues would have blamed Juliet for Romeo's.

There would have been a bloodbath. And besides, they weren't thinking of their families, so how could you call it a sacrifice? They didn't give a stuff about their families!

'You're all talking crap!' I shouted, standing up, scraping my chair on the floor. Everyone turned and stared at me. 'The whole stupid play's a load of rubbish!'

Ms de Rosa opened her mouth but no words came out. I felt like someone who's been at the top of a roller coaster waiting for the drop, and now it had started. It was picking up momentum. There was no stopping it.

'Romeo and Juliet are selfish and pathetic. They can't have what they want, so they're willing to throw everything away, like two spoilt kids, and they don't care who gets hurt!

'What about their parents and grandparents, and their brothers and sisters and uncles and aunts and cousins? What about their friends? What about the children they might have had one day, and the nieces and nephews? And the grandchildren? What do you reckon they would have thought of this scene?'

My heart was pounding so hard I could hardly

spit the words out. 'If you kill yourself,' I yelled, 'you might as well strap a load of Semtex to your body and invite all your friends and family round for tea. How can there be anything romantic, brave and beautiful about that?'

I could feel them all gawping at me but I didn't care. The roller coaster shook and rattled on down towards the abyss.

'If you kill yourself, you blow a huge hole in everything and your family falls in. Your mum goes weird, like her body's there but nobody's inside. Your dad gets drunk all the time and lashes out. Your brother turns into a scared little mouse, living in the garden because he doesn't want to come inside.

'Your sister... your sister...'

I remembered, suddenly, that night I walked home from Lexi's house after she'd dyed my hair, and everyone turned to look at me. It was such a buzz! I missed how I used to feel back then, before I became invisible.

The air was ringing with the sound of my voice. I wanted to leave, but I couldn't seem to move, because it was like my feet were frozen to the floor. Lexi got up out of her seat. She came over to me. Then she did an uncharacteristic thing. She hugged me.

Ms de Rosa wanted to speak to me at the end of the lesson but I slipped out while she was busy collecting up the homework, and hid in the toilets until they'd all moved on to History.

I got my coat and walked out of the building, still shaking with rage. I wanted to hit someone or break something or scream and shout the odds, but all I could do was walk and keep on walking.

I didn't have any kind of plan; I let my feet decide, and they marched along, thump, thump, thump on the pavements as if they had somewhere important to be.

As I strode past the minimart I thought about getting a bottle of vodka and necking it under a bush in the park. But my feet wouldn't stop and anyway, that would make me no better than Dad.

Thump, thump, thump, my feet pounded on, and I suddenly realised where they were heading. I could hear the traffic thundering along the dual carriageway, and I felt scared because what if my feet just kept on thump, thump, thumping and didn't stop?

I remembered that student last year who ran under the lorry on Hartley Hill. He was killed instantly, according to the news; he wouldn't have known a thing. The coroner said he must have been so deep in thought that he didn't even see the lorry barrelling down the hill, but seriously, how could you not notice a lorry?

My feet stopped briefly at the edge of the dual carriageway, and I could feel the whoosh of air from the cars racing by. Now, I was properly scared, but my feet decided to change direction and take the pavement alongside the road towards the footbridge.

Perhaps a person ought to trust their feet, I thought, watching them pace along. Even when you're distracted by thinking about implausibly short-sighted students, your feet know what they're doing and will find you a safe crossing.

We went up the ramp and onto the bridge. I didn't know the other side of the dual carriageway, so I was glad when my feet stopped in the middle. Maybe we were going to turn back now.

I looked down on the traffic streaming under me like fast water and imagined diving into it, and letting it sweep me away. I could easily climb up onto the barrier; my feet could do that, if they could get my hands to join in.

I put my hands in my pockets, and my fingers touched my phone. I brought it out, searched for Marigold's number, and pressed 'call'.

Marigold said, 'Jess? Where are you? Why aren't you in school?'

She said, 'I can hear traffic.'

She said, 'Talk to me, Jess!'

She sounded faint and far away, drowned out by the cars rushing under me.

I shouted down the phone at Marigold, 'You let it out, now make it go away!'

'Where are you Jess? I could meet you. Or if you come back to school, I can see you straight away.'

I pressed 'end'.

If there were angels, and you jumped off a high bridge, they might swoop down and catch your frightened soul, and lift it away, before your body got mashed like meat under the thundering wheels.

Lexi messaged me.

Are you all right?

She messaged me again.

Where are you? Why aren't you in History?

She bombarded me with messages.

Are you seeing Marigold? Have you gone home? Can I come over? Let me come over, I'll bunk off. What are you doing? Are you painting?

Painting. Yes, that was the thing. Now that Lexi had put the idea into my head, I knew where I had to be. It was me in charge, not my feet any more, as I strode back down off the bridge and headed home.

As soon as I stopped walking and started fumbling in my bag for my key, the shaking began again. I ran upstairs, pushed everything off my desk, and covered it with a big sheet of paper.

I lined up all my tubes of paint, filled my water pot, chose my brushes and then sat down looking at the blank sheet, waiting for a picture to come. But there didn't seem to be any pictures in my head. I squeezed some red paint out of the tube onto my mixing plate, added water and stirred it in.

I dropped a big blob of red on the paper, then another one. I stared at the two red blobs; round and shiny like big, thick drops of blood. I carefully

174

put down my brush, raised my arm, and smashed them with the side of my fist.

I squeezed more red paint straight onto the paper, worming and squirming, until the tube was completely empty. Then I smacked and splattered with my bare hands until nothing else existed, it was just me and the redness, which was like a living thing that I could pound and pummel until it was dead.

The paint splashed all the way up my arms and over my clothes. It spattered the walls and curtains. It spilled across the desk in a glistening sea of red and dripped down onto the carpet.

So much red! It wanted noise. I chose some music, docked my phone and turned the volume up as high as it would go, my wet, red fingers slipping and sliding on the buttons.

I could see then that my painting needed black; it needed black, bruise blue and purple. So I grabbed the tubes and squeezed them out and, using my flat hands as well as the sides of my fists, I slapped those colours down.

Now the yellow; now the green and the brown, now all the colours, I squeezed them onto the dark slick, like a pile of bright worms wriggling with life. Then I beat them down, down, down until there was nothing left of them and they had all turned to black.

I was staring down at my painting with the music thundering in my ears when Mum came in. They must have phoned her from school to say I'd gone missing.

She stood there blinking in the blast of noise, speechless at the state of my room.

'Go away!' I yelled. 'Leave me alone!'

She left, without even turning the music down, closing the door quietly behind her.

Suddenly feeling completely wiped out, I threw myself down on the bed, closed my eyes, and dropped like a stone into sleep.

I slept all day, until Mum came to wake me up for tea. The music had stopped, so maybe she'd been in earlier to turn it off, or maybe she'd just this minute done that before waking me up.

She didn't say anything at all about the fact that I was lying in bed covered in paint and my room was a total wreck.

'Tea's ready, Jess.'

'I don't want to come down.'

I was surprised that the words came out at all, let alone in my normal voice, not shouting. She seemed surprised too.

'That's all right. I can bring it up on a tray.'

But instead of going downstairs to get it, she kind of hovered, before finally sitting down on the edge of my bed.

'Would you like to talk?'

I shook my head.

'We're worried about you, Jess.'

We? Really? Some people had a funny way of showing it.

'I can't lose another child,' Mum said.

I don't know what everyone else had for tea, but Mum made me scrambled eggs and bacon which, as you know, is my favourite. I ate it in bed, balancing my laptop on my knees. I watched a really rubbish film about aliens and then another one about a serial killer who had a weird thing about cutlery.

At about eight o'clock, Mum came in to collect my empty tray; at nine o'clock she brought me some fresh sheets and offered to change my bed while I went in the shower. I shook my head and went on watching.

At ten o'clock she came to see if I wanted a late-night snack, and again at eleven to tell me she and Dad were going to bed. She said maybe I should go too, considering I had school in the morning.

But, having been asleep all day, I wasn't even slightly tired, so I went on watching films in my room, while the rest of the house creaked and sighed itself to sleep.

Acrylic paint dries like plastic, so you can paint over it almost immediately, unlike oils, which stay wet for weeks. Of course, if you pour it on thick, it takes longer to dry, and my painting had big pools of deeper paint that were still wet and glistening.

All my tubes of paint were squeezed empty and screwed up on the floor except the white one, which was lying on its own in the corner of the box. I took

177

my mixing plate and water pot to the bathroom, washed them, dried the plate with some tissue and filled the pot with clean water.

I squeezed some white paint onto the plate and mixed it with a few drops of water, using my favourite brush. I mixed and mixed, long after it was ready to use, just watching the sweep and swish of it.

I didn't actually want to paint. I wanted to see you. I wanted it so much. The book said when somebody close to you dies, at first it hurts like hell all the time, but then gradually you get little breaks in the pain, when maybe you can actually enjoy something.

As time goes on, the breaks get longer and the pangs of pain are more spaced out, but when they hit you, they still hurt just as much; it feels like your physical heart is breaking.

I wanted you to come into my room, the way you had when I was painting Tilly. I let the handle of my brush drop softly down onto the rim of the mixing plate and, leaving the bristles in the puddle of white, I sat back in my chair, to wait.

Marigold said you could forget, after someone dies, that you ever felt angry with them when they were alive. She said the best way to get in touch with your anger was simply to express it, and say how you feel.

When I told you what Mum had said after Dad pulled the potting shed down – that he wasn't a well man and that at least it had made him feel better – I suddenly thought, What about me? Do I not matter as much because I'm not ill? And that reminded me of how things had always been with you.

Your illness skewed our whole family life, because everything was geared up to protecting you from pain – you'd already had enough to deal with. Everyone had to be careful around you.

All my joys were secrets, because otherwise you might be jealous. All my problems were nothing compared with yours, which made me feel ashamed to even have them.

So when our teachers said you were cleverer, less moody and more sensible than me, I tried to be okay with that. I tried not to mind even when Mum and Dad did it too,

And when you swung it, knowing Mum wouldn't make you do your fair share, like the day you skived off clearing up after the party – I tried to tell myself it was funny and I didn't mind. But it wasn't funny. It chewed me up.

And when the Siblings Cancer Research doctor came to the house every couple of months to weigh and measure me and Marky, ask us questions and stick needles in our arms, I told myself, 'Suck it up'.

I mean, what was stripping down to your underwear and getting measured, compared with being stuck in hospital and having your foot cut off? Except, I'll tell you what it was; it was frightening. It kept reminding me that what happened to you might happen in our family again, and next time it might be me.

The white paint on my mixing plate was bone hard at the edges, and the brush would soon be stuck, but I left it there and went on waiting.

My mind reeled back to the very worst time, when you went away to hospital and didn't come back, and Mum was never at home, and Dad didn't want to be.

And Nan and Grampy pretended we were having a nice time, as if I was too young to understand what was going on or to see that, under the surface, all the grown-ups were out of their minds with worry.

Back then, I still thought it was all right to be angry and get upset, but I was just being difficult. You made me difficult, Seb, or rather, your illness did. That's what I would have told you, if you had been able to walk through my door.

Sitting there, in my bedroom, literally watching paint dry, I started to wonder what you might say back to me. I imagined our conversation.

You would say, perhaps, that it was the same for you, everyone behaving as if you were too young to understand what was going on. You would say, perhaps, that nobody ever asked you whether you wanted to have your foot cut off and be in hospital getting all those horrible treatments.

And you might say you never asked to be put on a pedestal like some kind of genius. Anyone who got stuck in bed for a year with nothing to do but read and surf the net is bound to look like a boffin, you might say.

Maybe you would say you weren't brilliant at all, and you knew it, and that was why you flunked your A-levels. The pressure to go to Cambridge was too much, you might say, and that was why you were smoking weed when you were supposed to be revising.

If you could come through that door and answer me back, you might say you never asked for preferential treatment, and you didn't like the way we pussy-footed round you.

I wanted to go on talking to you, so I lay down on my bed and shut my eyes, because then I couldn't see that you weren't there. I must have dozed for a couple of hours, before Mum and Dad's alarm woke me up at seven.

As I didn't want to see them, I crept downstairs to get some juice and cereal to take back to my room before they got up. I'd poured out the cereal and opened the fridge to look for milk, when Dad came down in his dressing gown. The way he stared at me made me realise I was still wearing my school uniform from yesterday, all splashed and splattered with paint.

'What the...? Uniform doesn't grow on trees,' he growled. 'Your mother and I have worked our fingers to the bone to give you kids everything you need...'

Blah blah blah.

I turned round to face him.

'Back off,' I said.

He stopped, astonished by the sound of my voice. When you're talking, you look at people's faces, and when I looked into his bloodshot eyes, after all this time, I felt like I really didn't know him.

Well, it's been a couple of weeks since I last wrote to you, Seb. Marigold's been bringing two new gels to every session, but I've been taking them back unused.

I've told Marigold I don't feel the need to write to you any more, now that I'm talking, but she says it would be better to say goodbye and sign off properly, and not just leave it hanging, because writing to you one last time would bring what she calls 'closure'.

When I started talking, things came out that I didn't even know were there, and some of them weren't very nice. I told Marigold maybe Dad wasn't the only one who hadn't loved you enough, but she shook her head. You couldn't measure love, she said.

Love didn't depend upon everything being nice, in fact it was quite the opposite. If everything was perfect between two people, love would be so easy that it wouldn't be worth a bean.

The point about love was that it could contain and survive all kinds of pain and imperfection. Anger, disappointment and blame were part of every relationship, and it was love's process to transform them.

'Transform them into what?' I asked.

'Forgiveness,' Marigold said.

In which case, I'll tell you who loves me a lot – Lexi. She's totally forgiven me for blanking her all that time. Of course, it's probably also helped that she's had a massive falling-out with her temporary bff Alyssa over the importance of designer labels.

This week, I've been round Lexi's house every day after school because Monk's in Romania and she's missing him like mad. Mum says it'll all end in tears, because he's too old to be going out with a schoolgirl, but she doesn't realise that Lexi isn't going to be at school much longer. As soon as she's legally allowed to, she's going to leave and get a job so she can save up and go travelling too.

She was telling me about it in her kitchen yesterday, as we munched our way through a bag of out-of-date doughnuts. There was never going to be an ideal time to tell her my news, so I just came out with it.

'I've missed four periods,' I said.

'Oh, my God!' she goes. 'We'd better go straight down the chemist's and get a pregnancy test.'

We were halfway down the road when I got this feeling and, just like magic, it was 'Hello, painters!' You'll be pleased to hear that, Seb, because even though you're dead, I'm sure you wouldn't like to think you had any family members related to that scumbag, Tris.

Telling Lexi the whole truth about what had happened with him was just the hardest thing. I hadn't even managed to talk to Marigold about it. If she'd asked,

I probably would have, but she didn't know anything about the sex quest and Tris, so why would she?

'Seb warned me,' I told Lexi, when we got back to her house and I'd sorted myself out. 'He told me what Tris was like, but I didn't want to hear it because I really liked him. I thought he was the one.'

'Well he was the one, in a way, the one you lost your virginity to, and that was always our plan.'

Plus it had been 'amazing', that was the word he'd used, Lexi said. So although Tris had turned out to be a scumbag for boasting about it afterwards and not using a condom, no real harm had been done.

In practical terms, I knew she was right, but she must have seen something else in my face because she said, 'What? What's wrong?'

'It wasn't amazing.'

I stopped, not knowing how to go on, but it was too late to turn back.

'Actually, it was horrible. I was really out of it and I didn't even know what was happening until he'd got my leg out of my jeans.'

I told Lexi I'd wanted him to stop but I couldn't say so, because his tongue was in my mouth, I could barely even breathe. Well, that was how it had seemed anyway, but maybe I really did want it to happen, because I was falling in love with him and after all, like she said, it had always been the plan to go all the way.

Lexi didn't say 'How could you be so stupid?' or anything like that. She looked really shocked.

'He raped you?' she said.

'What? No!' I shook my head. 'It was my own fault. I let him think it was what I wanted and then when I changed my mind, I was too drunk to say so.'

'Rape is never the victim's fault,' Lexi said slowly, leaning towards me and spreading the words out to make sure I heard every one.

I didn't want to think of myself as a victim. I was not a victim! 'I don't think it was rape,' I mumbled.

Lexi said yes, it was rape. Rape wasn't just about not saying no, it was also about not saying yes. If someone had sex with you without your consent, that was rape, and you couldn't give your consent if you were off your face

'But he knew I wanted to one day,' I said.

Lexi said she'd seen this thing online, that if you were confused about the question of consent, you had to imagine that instead of sex, someone was asking if you'd like a cup of tea.

Just because you thought you might like to have a cup of tea with them at some point in future, that didn't mean you were saying yes to this cup of tea right now. If you'd had tea with them in the past, it didn't mean you wanted to have a cup of tea with them again. You had to say yes or no to a cup of tea every time anyone asked.

'Except, obviously, when you're too drunk, and can't say anything at all,' Lexi said. 'And then they shouldn't even ask you. They should make sure you're okay and get you home safely, like any normal person would do who wasn't a rapist.'

I wished she would stop saying that word and yet, when she put it like that, it was all beginning to make sense, and seeing how shocked and upset she was about it made the way I'd been feeling seem less stupid and more, well, appropriate.

Lexi wanted to know all the details of that night, as far as I could remember, starting with the party. When I heard the words coming out of my mouth, it was like I was hearing it for the first time, and I understood what had happened with Tris in a completely different way.

I'd just finished the whole story when Lexi's mum came in, looking for her book, *To Love a Handsome Doctor*. Lexi's mum's got terrible taste in reading.

'Ah, there it is!' She pulled it out from behind the cushions. 'Would either of you like a cup of tea?'

We looked at each other, and laughed.

While Lexi's mum was rattling spoons and cups in the kitchen, Lexi asked me if I was going to go to the police. I shrugged. I was still getting my head round the fact that Tris had assaulted me.

'Well, whatever you decide, you can't let what happened with Tris put you off going out with guys and having sex,' Lexi said, 'because sex is the best thing ever. When me and Monk were doing it last time...'

No, no – stop it, Lexi – too much information!

Lexi says Monk's got this gorgeous cousin who

would be perfect for me, and we should all go out together. I said, 'One day, maybe,' because the thing is right now, it feels too soon.

'But feast your eyes,' goes Lexi, bringing up his profile. 'You know you want to!'

One of the good things about spending time at Lexi's is that it helps me keep out of Dad's way. Maybe he needs to stay in touch with his anger a little while longer, and then it will stop all on its own, or maybe the enquiry will go his way and he'll be able to go back to work, so at least he won't be in our faces 24:7.

But if things don't get any better, I'm going to see if I can move in with Lexi. We could both drop out of Sixth Form and get a job together. That would be all right.

Mum's always at work and Dad's usually drunk, so Nan's still coming round our house most afternoons. She sits cross-legged on the floor in my room and tries to talk to me about school etc, but I don't see the point. She's the last person I'd go to now if I needed advice.

She cooks the tea and gets us all sitting down together, but it isn't like it used to be. Dad might say something about a story in the news, and Mum will just nod or shake her head. Even though I'm talking again, I don't join in.

Marky plays with Digger under the table, and gives him scraps when he thinks nobody's looking. The conversation doesn't go anywhere, no one raises their voice, nothing matters that much any more.

JENNY ALEXANDER

Back then, when you were here, we'd have all been shouting the odds, Dad going on about God or the government, Mum serving up the food and lecturing us about healthy eating, you throwing in some obscure thing you'd been reading, and Marky constantly trying to change the subject and talk about football.

Tilly would be lying in her basket, keeping an eye out for falling titbits. Life was really good, only we just didn't notice it.

Marky's moved back in from the annexe now the weather's got colder. He hasn't grown, but he seems older. He used to be the baby of the family, but now he's just the younger one of two.

I read somewhere that losing someone close to you is like losing a limb – you adjust, but it never feels right again. It will never feel right to me, a born-and-bred middle child, to have no older brother or sister.

On the dresser, there are photos of us all in school uniform, or playing on the beach at Holkham, or messing around in the garden. I'm going to choose one soon and copy it. I might show it to my tutor when Saturday classes start again at the Art School after Christmas.

I still don't know why you did it. If I'd known you were going to, I would have watched for signs, but it's not the kind of thing you think you have to do. Even when you see a big sign like that box of stolen tablets, it's easy to miss it, because you don't know what it means; you don't understand that it's deadly serious.

188

You were my big brother, Seb; you had always been there and I assumed you always would be there, forever. I could never have imagined, back then, that I would ever have to live without you.

You didn't seem unhappy or depressed to me. You didn't even seem bored. And what Marigold says about it being a single terrible moment – that doesn't sound like you at all. Maybe a hothead like Romeo would react without thinking, but you weren't like that. You were a calm and serious person.

It seems to me that, in some ways, silence is like suicide. It makes you invisible and removes you from the world. It confuses people, and hurts the ones that love you. It takes you far, far out from the ebb and flow of normal life, to a place where everything feels unfamiliar and nothing looks the same.

I don't know how or why I drifted out there. And maybe that's the way it was for you. Maybe it's not always a moment, like Marigold says, but a tide you can stray into, and nothing can stop it, and no one can save you.

I'm so sorry, Seb, that it carried you away. And I'm so grateful that it brought me back to shore.

With love always
From your sister
Jess x

Recommended Websites

If you have been affected by any of the issues in this book, don't suffer in silence. There are many organisations that can offer help and support.

In the UK, these include:

www.hopeagain.org.uk
This is the youth website for Cruse, the UK's leading bereavement charity, www.cruse.org.uk. It offers a safe place for young people who are facing grief to share their stories with others.

https://www.papyrus-uk.org
Help and advice for young people who are thinking about suicide, or for anyone worried about a young person who might be

https://www.thecalmzone.net
Help and support for men of any age in the UK who may be considering suicide

http://www.winstonswish.org.uk
Support for bereaved children and young people and their families

http://www.childline.org.uk
Confidential counselling for children and young people up to age 19

http://uk-sobs.org.uk
Support for adult survivors of bereavement by suicide

http://www.samaritans.org
Help for anyone who feels depressed, distressed or suicidal

http://www.rapecrisis.org.uk
Information about how to get help if you have been sexually assaulted or raped

If you don't live in the UK, you can find organisations in your own area by doing a simple internet search for suicide, bereavement, youth counseling or rape crisis helplines.

Acknowledgements

I would like to thank all the friends who have read the manuscript of this book through its various versions and given me such helpful feedback and encouragement, particularly my very first reader, Ian Alexander, and my very last, Daisy Newth.

Printed in Great Britain
by Amazon